Murder Is Medical

A Susan Wiles Schoolhouse Mystery

by
Diane Weiner

For information, email **Cozy Cat Press**, cozycatpress@aol.com or visit our website at: www.cozycatpress.com

ISBN: 978-1-946063-67-0

Printed in the United States of America

1 2 3 4 5 6 7 8 9 10

This book is dedicated to the medical school professors and staff of Washington University in St. Louis, Missouri. Thank you for the love and hard work you invest in creating the next generations of medical professionals.

Chapter 1

"What if he doesn't get the residency he wants? What if he and Cara don't get to stay together?" Susan Wiles felt the perspiration creep up her neck, and she was at least a decade beyond blaming it on menopause. She pulled off her wool scarf and with some effort, stuffed it between her body and the armrest. Not exactly roomy, but better than the airplane seat she had to tolerate for the three-hour flight from New York to St. Louis last night. Her sides were still sore from where the armrests dug into her. She pushed her bifocals up and opened the program, scanning it for Evan's name.

"He and Cara have been at the top of the class all the way through. I'm sure it will work out just fine," said Mike. He grabbed his wife's soft, fleshy hand. Their daughter, Lynette, and her husband Jason filled out the row, sandwiching their two granddaughters. The younger one, Mia, began to fuss. Susan pulled a graham cracker out of her purse and was about to offer it, when Lynette pushed her hand away.

Annalise, the older sister, looked just like Lynette did at that age, right down to the golden blond pigtails. She would be starting kindergarten in the fall and knew her way around a laptop like nobody's business. At the moment, she was mesmerized watching the people coming into the auditorium and the stage crew fussing with the microphones.

Susan bet her bottom dollar that one day they'd watch Annalise graduate medical school, or take the presidential oath of office. Either would be safer than law enforcement, their mother's profession.

The house lights lowered and the dean of the medical school took the stage.

"Welcome to our annual Match Day ceremony." He explained the procedure. One by one, or as a couple, if the students had agreed they wanted to stay together for residency, names would be randomly announced. The student would come to the stage, take his envelope from the class advisor, and read the results to the audience.

Dr. Schmidt, fiftyish, with dark hair and a bit of a belly, took the microphone. He joked, drawing a parallel to the Oscars, as he called the first name—a not so subtle attempt at relieving the tension. Following tradition, some students were dressed in silly costumes. Evan had warned her about that. One was accompanied by his wife dressed as a dinosaur, another wore a Superman cape. Her hands hurt from grasping the seat so hard. Finally, Dr. Schmidt called, "Evan Wiles and Cara Martin."

Susan fumbled with the camera on her phone. Why hadn't she gone ahead and done that online phone photography class? She first focused on Cara, long, silky hair falling over her fit and flare blue satin dress, and held down the red button. She watched a professional photographer snapping pictures in front of the stage, and felt relieved that the moment would be captured, even if she screwed up the photo.

Cara tore open her envelope. "Pediatrics, right here at St. Agnes." She gave a squeal.

Evan opened his. Susan held her breath. "Radiology, also here at St. Agnes."

Susan had secretly hoped they'd wind up closer to home in New York, but they'd both gotten their first choices, and she was thrilled that they'd be together.

The audience clapped, and Evan hugged Cara. His friends gave him high fives as he returned to his seat.

Mike whispered, "We did good."

Susan felt like a peacock fanning her feathers as she put her phone in her purse. "I tried to video it. Hope it came out."

"Got you covered, Mom." Lynette held up her phone.

Susan thought back to Evan in middle school, when he fell in love with Biology class. Then high school, shadowing their family physician, and a college summer spent volunteering in Honduras. She hadn't slept nights after she heard the country had been dubbed the murder capital of the world. It all added up to this…Evan becoming a doctor.

After the ceremony concluded, they snapped a picture of their son on the way out of the auditorium. In the lobby, Evan introduced them to Dr. Schmidt.

"Congratulations. Evan is going to do great things. He did a rotation under me but I couldn't persuade him to go into psychiatry."

Talk about dangerous professions! She was glad he hadn't been successful in his attempt. Dr. Schmidt had a warm smile and Susan detected a dimple or two.

"Thanks for all you've done for him. Evan and Cara raved about the training they received in all areas," said Susan.

"My wife and I are hosting a reception at our place tonight. An open house of sorts. The kids got invites. Hope to see you there." He looked to Lynette and Jason. "The girls are welcome, too." He popped a piece of gum into his mouth. "Trying to quit smoking, for the hundredth time."

"Thanks," said Lynette.

"We'll be there," said Mike.

Cara's mother, on a mission, said "Come on, Evan. Stand next to Cara." They took turns taking pictures in every possible combination, with Susan and Mike getting in on the action as well.

"Are you going to the reception tonight?" asked Cara's mom.

Susan fumbled getting her arms into her coat sleeves. "Wouldn't miss it."

On the way to the car, they ran into Wes Jacobs, Evan's roommate.

"Congratulations! I bet you're excited about starting residency next year."

Evan nudged Susan in the ribs.

"Not what I'd expected, but thank you."

Once in the car, Evan said, "You shouldn't have said that. Wes is really upset. He didn't even match at first. One of the professors made a few calls and got him into the program at North Dakota Memorial. He isn't happy."

"I didn't see his parents."

"He told his mom not to come. His father died when he was in elementary school."

"Why wouldn't he have matched?"

"He's struggled with the book work. Didn't do well on the first part of his medical licensing exam, either. He's good with the patients, though."

"That's too bad, but in the end, wherever he does his residency, he'll still be a doctor when he graduates in May."

"That's true. He'll get over it in time."

Chapter 2

After a celebratory lunch at Evan's favorite restaurant, Susan spent most of the afternoon napping. The calzones sat like a rock in her stomach and she felt like doing little else. When she awoke, it was time to head to the reception.

Mike maneuvered the rental Kia through the Italian section of St. Louis.

"This area's called University City. Turn left at the corner," said Evan. "We ate dinner at that place with Cara's parents." He pointed out the window.

"I love brick houses," said Susan, as they rode through a residential area. She'd been impressed with St. Louis all along and as they passed lights in the windows, and smoke puffing from chimneys, she imagined the cozy residents inside, eating at solid wood tables with stone fireplaces roaring in the living room.

Rain began to pound the windshield just as they arrived at Dr. Schmidt's 'mansion.' She pictured Cara and Evan living in a place like this down the road and wondered if it had a guest house in back to accommodate visiting grandparents.

"I've got two little umbrellas in my purse," said Susan. It didn't stop the rain from blowing onto her clothes and giving her a chill. The men made a run for the overhang.

Gail Schmidt, stylish silver hair accented by a teal blue silk blouse, answered the door.

"Welcome. Come on in and help yourself."

Susan wiped her feet vehemently on the mat, afraid to leave marks on the sparkling white tile floor. Champagne-colored candles glowed on the buffet table and the house smelled of cinnamon. A fancier affair than she'd anticipated, Susan wished she'd put on a dress instead of her standard uniform of stretchy black pants and a sweater.

Neil Schmidt approached, putting his arm on his wife's shoulder. "Glad you made it. Grab a drink."

He led them to the buffet, where they got in line behind a gangly teenage boy wearing jeans and an untucked shirt.

"This is my son, Brian."

Susan said, "Nice to meet you, Brian. Going to follow in your father's footsteps?"

"Nope." He glared at his father with steely eyes.

Susan felt the tension, like water against oil between father and son.

Neil said, "Brian's more the artistic type. Right, son?" He popped a piece of gum into his mouth, shoving the wrapper back in his pocket. "Although he *was* acing Chemistry and Physics when he changed his schedule to be in drawing class."

"Whatever." Brian rolled his eyes, grabbed his plate and walked off into the next room.

Evan high-fived his roommate, Wes Jacobs, and a handsome chocolate-skinned man she didn't recognize.

"Mom and Dad, this is Boston Talmich. He's a third year psych resident. He's doing research with Dr. Schmidt, but don't ask him what kind of research. If he tells you he'll have to kill you."

"Hardly top secret. Just waiting to see if it pans out before we jump the gun. I'm starving, let's get some food." He got behind them in the buffet line.

Susan scoped out the choices—steamed asparagus, grilled eggplant, a luscious salad—healthy eating was an option. Just not the option she chose.

Scooping out mounds of food, Susan glanced at Mike's plate. "Sliders and deep fried shrimp? The cardiologist told you no fried foods and limited amounts of lean beef." The buns were shiny, and with the spackling of batter on the shrimp, she could barely make out what was underneath.

"And what about you? Mini cheesecakes, two brownies, and a chocolate éclair? Not to mention a second glass of champagne. I'm sure your blood sugar is going to go sky high. Come on. We're on vacation." He led her into the living room, where Cara and her parents were seated. The warmth from the brick fireplace caressed Susan's damp pant legs as she downed a glass of champagne.

"How was *Sauce on the Side*?" Cara sipped mineral water from a crystal flute.

Susan had forgotten that Cara grew up in St. Louis. Her parents moved to Chicago only recently. "I'm still stuffed," said Susan, about to grab a canapé as the waiter walked past. Her blood sugar *had* been a disaster lately. If she didn't keep herself on track with her type two diabetes she'd have to go on medication. She pulled back her hand.

Cara's mother said, "I forgot Boston Talmich was doing his residency here."

"So you know him?"

"He was a few years ahead of Cara in school, same grade as my son. His family moved to California after he graduated. Your son's roommate went to the same school too." She nodded towards Wes Jacobs. "His family has been through a lot."

"What do you mean?"

"The father died when the boys were young. After that, Wes's brother, Jake, was always in trouble. He was even arrested a few times, quite the opposite of Wes. Wes was top of the class and a track star to boot. Anyway, there was a terrible fire when the boys were in college. Jake died, and it was a long road to recovery for Wes and his Mother. Wes was in the burn unit for months."

"How awful. His mother must be very proud of him now."

Susan looked at Boston Talmich across the room. He crumpled something in his hand, then walked past and threw it into the fireplace. *What was that all about? Surely he could have found a trash can.* He stopped to chat with Cara and her parents, then turned when a petite woman with a deep velvet voice said, "Congratulations to you all." The deep voice coming from this tiny woman was incongruous.

"Dr. Potter, I didn't see you come in. These are Evan's relatives, and I think you met Cara's parents. Dr. Potter is head of psychiatry at St. Agnes." Boston took a sip of his wine.

Judith Potter was smartly dressed in a silk pant suit, accentuated with pearls. Her face was youthful, but the wrinkled hands wrapped around the champagne flute indicated she was near Susan's age.

"Mr. and Mrs. Wiles, I had the pleasure of working with Evan during his psychiatry rotation last year. I hear he's staying at St. Agnes for residency."

"Yes," said Susan. "It was his first choice and we're thrilled for him."

Dr. Schmidt passed by, drink in hand. "Judith, I'm pleased you came."

"These were my students, too. I wouldn't miss it and let you claim all the credit for training them. If you'll excuse me, I haven't said hello to Gail yet."

After Dr. Potter and Dr. Schmidt walked away, Boston explained, "Those two are arch rivals. I'm surprised they're even speaking to each other."

"Rivals?" said Susan.

"Judith Potter got the head of psychiatry position at the hospital, which everyone expected would go to Dr. Schmidt. And then there's the issue of funding. There are only so many research dollars to go around."

Dr. Schmidt clinked a spoon on his champagne glass. "I'd like to propose a toast to this extraordinary group of future doctors and the families who helped them get here. Congratulations and Happy Match Day." The clinking of glass on glass filled the room.

Susan and Mike mingled and met some of Evan's other teachers and classmates. Mia had fallen asleep in Jason's arms and Annalise was getting cranky. Lynette suggested heading back to the hotel.

"I'm going to run to the rest room and then we can go," said Susan. She squeezed Mike's arm. Her eyes felt heavy and she was ready to crawl into bed. She couldn't help peeking into every room as she found her way to the bathroom. *A Steinway. I wonder if any of them play or if it's just for show.*

The bathroom itself was pristine, with gold-toned fixtures and a double marble sink. Floating tea candles on the vanity filled the bathroom with a vanilla scent. *I'll bet they never use this bathroom except for parties.* In contrast, the downstairs bathroom at Chez Wiles had a cracked vanity and no matter how often she swept, cat litter from Johann and Ludwig's box in the corner was perpetually sprinkled across the linoleum floor.

When she finished bathing her hands with lavender soap and smoothing on a bit of the coordinating hand lotion, she flicked off the light. Standing in the hall, she froze when she heard footsteps and caught a glimpse of someone disappearing behind a door. *Was that the study?* She thought so, but after a couple of glasses of champagne she couldn't be certain. She returned to the living room in time to see Dr. Schmidt stumbling across the room.

"I, I just wanted to, just wanted to…" He collapsed on the ground with a thud, knocking food off the buffet table.

His wife ran to his side and screamed. "Someone help."

Dr. Potter ran to his side, gave his airways a quick check, and then started CPR. "Call 911."

"Is he breathing?" said Gail. Evan knelt beside Judith Potter and shook his head.

"Does he have a heart condition?" asked Dr. Potter.

"No. He goes to the gym. He's never sick."

"Allergies?" Dr. Potter pumped her hands ferociously on Dr. Schmidt's chest.

Brian, the teenager they'd met earlier, ran into the room. "What's going on?"

Dr. Potter, out of breath, told Brian, "Get my keys out of my purse and get my bag from my car."

Susan remembered the jade green Versace bag Judith came in with and rifled through it for the keys. She tossed them to Brian.

"Which car?" Brian's fists were clenched and he had the look of a lost toddler in the midst of Macy's on Black Friday.

"The (*pump*) black…Audi. At (*pump*) the end of the driveway."

As if someone had thrown cold water in his face, Brian came to life and sprinted out the front door.

Boston Talmich knelt beside Neil Schmidt. "Let me take over. You're exhausted." He relieved Judith Potter, pumping Dr. Schmidt's chest with fresh strength.

"Where's Brian? I have epinephrine in my bag."

It had been only minutes since the collapse but time moved like molasses. Gail cried out, "Where's that ambulance? Are they lost?"

"No," said Susan. How could they miss this McMansion with all the lights on and a street full of cars in front? She looked at her watch. As best as she remembered, she calculated the trip from here to the hospital. Even if they'd flown the ambulance wouldn't yet be here.

Lynette placed Annalise on the sofa next to Jason, holding Mia. "I'll go out front and make sure they see us."

"Should I call again?" asked Cara.

Brian returned carrying a black bag. Dr. Potter opened it and readied a syringe. Evan rolled up Dr. Schmidt's sleeve and Judith stuck him with the needle.

"Did it work?" asked Gail.

Sirens crescendoed as the ambulance approached the house. Flashing red light shone through the front window.

"Thank God," said Gail.

The following minutes were a blur. A metal stretcher screeched across the tiled foyer. Boston Talmich moved aside. An EMT hooked up a portable defibrillator while another stuck the doctor with more epinephrine.

"Clear." They waited. No heartbeat. Another shot of epi. The EMT's tried again. "Clear."

"Is he okay?" said Gail. Brian hugged his mom as they watched the scene. The commotion stopped. The house was quiet, holding its collective breath. The EMTs worked relentlessly for what felt like hours. One shook his head.

Dr. Potter's voice broke the silence. "I'm so sorry, but, I'm afraid he's gone."

Chapter 3

Morning came too soon. Between the horror of watching Dr. Schmidt die in front of them, and too much champagne, only the threat of the free breakfast buffet coming to an end nudged her out of bed. Mike had already showered and was checking his mail on his phone.

"Sleep okay?"

"Not really. Poor Mrs. Schmidt and her son. Imagine what they must be going through."

Lynette and Jason were already seated when she and Mike arrived.

"Grandma, can I have one of your doughnuts?" asked Annalise.

Susan looked to Lynette for approval before replying. "Sure, sweetie. I'll bet you want the one with the sprinkles, right?"

"Mom, a detective called this morning and asked if we'd go down to the station. She wants to interview whoever was at the reception last night."

"Why? He died from a heart attack, right?"

"There were a few red flags, they just want to be thorough."

"Oh, you mean like how was it possible an overweight, middle-aged man had a heart attack while drinking champagne?" She glared at her husband. "Are they thinking he was murdered?"

"Leave it to you, Mom. Every death isn't murder."

"And if it turns out to be murder, this time we won't be here long enough for you to stick your nose in," said Mike.

"That's right. And just because they found traces of a mysterious substance in his cup, it doesn't mean someone killed him."

"A mysterious substance?" Susan's eyes widened. "His champagne flute?"

"No. It's nothing." Lynette put more scrambled eggs on Mia's high chair tray. "When you're ready, we can go together. Jason will stay with the girls and stop by later."

After breakfast, Susan filled up a take-out coffee cup and shook out a few Excedrin from the bottle in her purse before heading to the elevator. She tried not to look at the guests in the fitness room as they walked past. *Who goes away and brings exercise clothes? They'd stink up the whole suitcase on the way home.* Back in her room, she exchanged the black stretchy pants she had on for a newer pair.

"Mike, when I went to the bathroom, someone was down the hall. I saw someone sneak into the study."

"You had a few drinks last night. Are you sure it wasn't Gail or the son?"

"Gail was in the living room when I returned. Brian, the son, came in later, right when Gail was screaming. And he and his father didn't get along; you witnessed that conversation yourself."

"He's a teenager. You remember how it was when Lynette and Evan were that age. Teenagers are always mad at their parents over something. It was a heart attack. Plain and simple."

"I wonder what the police found."

Lynette texted that she was downstairs waiting.

"Saved by the bell," said Mike.

The morning rush hour had cleared. The famous arch was more visible than it had been yesterday, now that the clouds were gone.

"Next time we visit, Jason wants us to take the girls to a Cardinals game. I wonder if they'd have any interest by then."

"You loved when I took you to see the Mets," said Mike. "I think we started going when you were around Annalise's age."

"I never told you, but I only went for the ice cream in the little plastic helmet."

When they arrived at the local police station, they were met by an attractive, honey-skinned detective around Lynette's age.

"Detective Jazmin Lowe." She shook their hands. "Detective Greene, I'm the one you spoke to on the phone. We're going to go ahead and open an investigation."

"What did you find at the house?" said Susan.

Detective Lowe ignored her.

"Did you find any rat poison in the pantry?"

Lynette mouthed 'sorry.'

Detective Lowe turned to Susan and Mike. "And you're Detective Greene's parents. Mrs. Wiles, your daughter told me all about you. You're first."

Susan followed Detective Lowe into the interview room. She was expecting the windowless, cold cell with a metal table and chair like she'd seen on TV so many times, but instead was ushered into a cozy office.

"Is that a picture of your son?" asked Susan.

"Yes, Elijah. Just turned eight. Now, tell me your version of what happened last night."

Susan tried to remember details. "Guests were in and out all evening, but when Dr. Schmidt died, his wife was in the living room beside him. His son, Brian, was not in the room. He came in when his mother screamed."

"Did you see where he came in from?"

She wasn't sure. "I saw someone come out of the study which was in the same hallway as the bathroom. I don't know for a fact it was him. There was a staircase. I suppose the bedrooms were upstairs so maybe he'd been in his room."

"Mrs. Wiles, just stick with what you saw. He came from the hallway where the bathroom was on the first floor."

"Yes."

"Keep going. Who else was in the room?"

"Cara, that's my son Evan's girlfriend, and her family were there, as were Evan and his roommate, Wes."

"Wes?" She looked through her notes. Wesley Jacobs?"

"Yes. Evan and he have been roommates from the start. He's going into cardiology, just got a residency in North Dakota. Not where he wanted to be. I was hoping Evan would wind up in New York, but…"

Detective Lowe cleared her throat.

"Yes, I know. Just the facts," said Susan. This wasn't her first rodeo. She'd heard those same words before. "And the psych resident, Boston Talmich was in the living room. And Dr. Potter had just arrived. Judith Potter. She's a psychiatrist just like Dr. Schmidt is—was. Boston said they didn't get along."

"Did he share why that was the case?"

"Something about competition."

"What did you see right before Dr. Schmidt collapsed?"

"Nothing unusual. He'd given a toast a few minutes before he collapsed. If it wasn't a heart attack, I'll bet he was poisoned."

"I never said it wasn't a heart attack."

"The killer had to be present. Otherwise, how could he be sure the poison made it to the correct target?"

"No one said he was poisoned."

"Did you check the garage? Antifreeze tastes sweet and could have been mixed into the champagne."

"Thank you, Mrs. Wiles."

"If you need anything else, we're staying at the Holiday Inn. We'll be here a few more days."

Detective Lowe ushered Susan out of the office. "Isn't your husband here?"

"He must have gone for a cup of coffee. He'll be right back, I'm sure." She sat in a plastic seat outside the office, where Boston Talmich was waiting.

Detective Lowe brought Boston Talmich into her office. The door hadn't completely shut and Susan inched as close as possible. Lynette must have gone with Mike. She hung on every word she heard.

"Mr. Talmich, what's your relation to Dr. Schmidt?" said Detective Lowe.

"I'm a psychiatry resident. I've worked with him on various research projects and he's been a mentor."

"Did the doctor have any enemies as far as you know?"

"I heard him arguing with Dr. Potter the day before yesterday. They were screaming at each other out in the parking lot. Are you saying he didn't die of a heart attack?"

"What were they arguing about?"

"I heard Dr. Potter say it was about to hit the fan. He said something like '*over my dead body.*' Then I heard her mumble something about going to jail as she went to her car. He and Dr. Potter had history. They hated each other. I was surprised to see her at the reception."

"What was the source of that tension?"

"They are both respected researchers. Rumor is it had to do with their work. Dr. Potter had an issue with Dr. Schmidt not following proper protocol."

Boston Talmich said he was surprised to see Dr. Potter, however, she was the first one to come to Dr. Schmidt's rescue and try to save him when he collapsed. Was it all an act? She had arrived shortly before the toast. Did she have a chance to gain access to the bottle of champagne? Motive, professional competition, check. Means…she is a doctor. She'd know how to induce a heart attack.

She heard the chairs move inside the office and scooted away, grabbing her phone and pretending to read. A minute later, Detective Lowe and Boston Talmich emerged, not noticing her.

"You might look at his son, too," added Boston.

"Why's that?"

"He used to stop by every now and then, but I haven't seen him in months before the night of the party. Dr. Schmidt made a comment a while back about hating traffic as much as his son hated him. Thought that was weird."

"Teenagers say they hate their parents all the time."

"I guess, but something about the look on his face, the tone of his voice. I don't know."

A heavy-set black woman barged into the waiting area. "Jazmin, I brought you a muffin. I stopped and got one for Elijah before school and I know how you forget to eat breakfast all the time."

"Thanks. This is my mom, Valerie. Mom, Susan Wiles and Boston Talmich."

"Nice to meet you," said Susan.

Lynette came around the corner. "Mom, are you and Dad done yet?"

Detective Lowe said, "Your mom's done, but we're waiting on your father. Detective Greene, this is *my* mom. She looks out for me."

"And I help her solve cases, isn't that right, Jazzy?"

Detective Lowe shook her head. "Yes, Mom. Couldn't do my job without you."

Susan said, "I help Lynette solve cases all the time, too."

"Yes, said Lynette. "Like two peas in a pod." She rolled her eyes.

"Here's Dad now."

Mike handed Susan a coffee. "Are you ready for me, Detective?"

"Yes, come on in." She closed the door behind her.

"Mom, I'm going back to the hotel to pack. We're leaving in the morning, remember."

"Yes, Lynette. "It'll take us no time at all to pack. I'll call you when we leave here."

Susan plopped back down in the plastic chair. Valerie sat next to her.

"Want a muffin to go with that coffee?" said Valerie. She handed Susan a jumbo chocolate chip muffin from the white paper bag she had stashed in her oversized purse.

"I'm supposed to be watching my sugar, but the murder has knocked me for a loop." She peeled away the white wrapper.

Valerie grabbed an identical muffin from the bag. "Same here. Don't tell Jazmin you saw me eating this."

A kindred spirit. If they lived in the same town, she had a hunch they'd be friends. "I saw a picture of your grandson on her desk. He's adorable."

"He's my little honey, Elijah. Jazmin thinks I'm helping her out, but truth is, he helps me. I lost my husband not too long before Nick died."

"I'm sorry for your loss," said Susan. "I can't imagine how hard that must have been, both for you and Jazmin."

"No, until you lose your husband, you really can't imagine how lonely and sad you feel. After Elijah's daddy died, I retired from my job as an office manager and stepped in to help. With the hours Jazmin keeps, she can't always pick up Elijah from school or his activities. It was four years ago, but sometimes I stay over when she works late and I hear Jazmin crying in her bedroom. Nick was one of the good ones. I miss him myself. We both talk about him a lot around Elijah, to keep his memory alive. You got grandkids?"

"Do I have grandkids? Two granddaughters. Annalise just turned five, and Mia is two and a half." She pulled her phone from her purse and unlocked it. "See. There they are."

"Beautiful girls. The little blondie has your eyes. What brings you to St. Louis?"

Susan smiled. "My son, Evan, graduates medical school in May. We're in town for Match Day, where the students find out where they go for their residencies."

"I overheard Jazmin talking about the murder last night. Says it happened at a reception at a doctor's house."

She's referring to it as murder? "Yeah. We were there. The poor guy proposes a toast, drinks some champagne, and a while later, boom, he's gone."

"So he was poisoned?" Valerie crossed her arms as if that was a substantiated conclusion.

"Don't know. We assumed it was a heart attack."

"They wouldn't be bringing you all here if it was that simple. Knowing Jazzy, she has a suspect list already."

"The only two names I can imagine are on it at this point are a rival researcher, and his own son." Susan was enjoying this discussion.

"His son?"

"Well, according to the guy who your daughter just interviewed anyway."

Mike stepped through the door. "I'm all done. Detective Lowe says we can go and to call if we remember anything else. She gave me her card."

"Valerie, nice to meet you, and thanks for the muffin."

"Likewise. Where is home?"

"Westbrook, New York. It's a small town in the Hudson Valley."

"Then have a good trip back to New York."

Chapter 4

Susan felt a familiar emptiness whenever she had to say goodbye to her son. They'd gone out to dinner with Evan and Cara last night. At least this time they'd be back for graduation in less than two months. She closed her suitcase and took a swig of the hotel coffee she'd made in the Keurig. It was too early for the free breakfast, but they'd have time to grab something at the airport.

"Mike, come on. Wake up, we're going to be late."

Her phone lit up. She texted back to Lynette. *We'll meet you downstairs in twenty minutes.* "Mike, I know you're packed but it's time to get up." She shook his shoulder.

"I can't. My arm is killing me, and my chest hurts really bad."

Mike had suffered a heart attack a few years ago and Susan's stomach dropped. "Is it your heart?"

"Call 911, now."

Her fingers were shaking. She dialed 911. "It's my husband. He's having a heart attack," She knocked the coffee onto the floor, hardly noticing. "Hurry. Yes, he's breathing but not for long if you don't send that ambulance right now."

Her thoughts felt like they were wrapped in fog. Last night, Neil Schmidt collapsed from a supposed heart attack, and now her husband? Was this really a coincidence? She called Lynette, who banged on the door less than five minutes later.

"Dad, can you sit up?"

"No, I can barely move. My chest is killing me."

Lynette called the front desk to alert them which room to direct the ambulance to. "Dad, it's going to be okay. We're around the corner from St. Agnes. The ambulance will be here soon."

Susan grabbed her phone. "Evan, it's Mom. Dad is having a heart attack. Meet us at the hospital." She heard sirens. By the time she ended the call, the EMTs were at the door. They piled him on to a stretcher and hooked up a monitor in the blink of an eye.

"Mom, go with the ambulance. I'll meet you at the emergency room."

Susan longed to squeeze Mike's hand during the ambulance ride, but stayed out of the way of the EMTs who were busy attending to Mike. *I should have insisted he keep up with his exercise. I'm a terrible enabler. Just last week when Mike was about to ride the stationary bike I suggested going to Denny's.*

The last time they had to rush back to the hospital was during their Atlanta trip, but luckily, that turned out to be indigestion. She wished that was the current situation, but the way they were attending to Mike, she knew it wasn't. Losing Mike was her biggest fear. He was her best friend. Just yesterday she met Jazmin Lowe and her mother Valerie, both widowed, and now there was Gail Schmidt, poor thing. How did they manage to go on?

The ambulance screeched to a stop in front of the emergency entrance. Mike was whisked away, while Susan was handed a clipboard full of forms to fill out. The door flew open.

"Mrs. Wiles, what's going on?" said Wes. "Does Evan know you're here?"

"I...I don't know. Mike's having a heart attack. I wish they'd let me go back there."

"Wow, I just saw him last night when you came by to pick up Evan for dinner. I'll see what I can find out. I'm finishing my cardiology rotation."

The door flew open again.

"Mom, any news?" said Lynette. Her hair was mussed and her shirt misbuttoned. It took a lot to rankle Lynette, but the possibility of her father dying did it.

"They were working on him the whole ride over and whisked him back as soon as we got here. Evan's roommate is trying to get some news for me. Did you see Evan?"

"Not yet."

"Our flight? And we're supposed to check out of the hotel."

"Don't worry about that now. Jason's there with the girls and he'll take care of it."

Susan paced back and forth. "Why can't I be with him?"

"What are those? Do you need to fill those out?"

Susan picked up the clipboard. "I started to but I can't focus."

Evan ran into the waiting room and hugged her. "Mom, any news yet?"

"No. Wes is trying to find out what's happening. Why can't I be with him?"

"Let them do their evaluating and figure out what's going on. Then they'll let you see him."

"What if this is it? We cheated death the first time, but he fell back into old habits and this is his punishment. My punishment for not keeping him on track."

"That's ridiculous. He was at risk regardless because of his prior history."

"You say that, but I know what you're thinking. Last time you came home remember how you sat me down and said I had to get serious with my diabetes and Dad's heart. Remember?"

"Mom, this isn't your fault. You called for help right away and he was still conscience when the EMTs got there, right?"

"Yes."

Wes came back through the door. "They're finishing some tests, then you'll be able to see him."

"Is he in pain?"

"No, they gave him something for the pain. Do you have those forms? They need the medical history and his doctor's contact info."

Susan quickly scribbled in the information she could. Wes ran it back.

Evan said, "You got him here right away. It's going to be okay."

Lynette got coffee from the machine and handed it to her mother. "Dad's a fighter. No way is he going to die before he sees his son graduate med school, you know that, right?"

Thank God she had her children with her. She squeezed Lynette's hand. You take care of them all those years while they're growing up and then they take care of you. She couldn't imagine going through this alone. *God, thank you for Lynette and Evan. Please, please, don't let them lose their father.* Although a sporadic church goer, during times of crisis, she fell back on her faith.

"Mrs. Wiles?"

Susan read the badge hanging from the young doctor's neck. *Stephan Cushing, MD, Cardiology.* "I'm Susan Wiles."

"Your husband needs surgery. There's a blockage and we need to do a cardiac bypass."

"And then he'll be fine?"

"All surgery comes with risk, but if we don't operate, you're looking at a negative outcome. If you'll sign this consent form, we'll get him prepped."

"Can I see him?"

"For a few minutes. Come on back."

Susan followed the doctor to where Mike was. The monitors beeped like a ticking time bomb and an IV tethered him to the bed. She trembled looking at him.

"Some way to extend our vacation and not have to go back to work," said Susan.

"Yeah. They put me in the penthouse suite. Rumor is they're serving gourmet Jell-O for lunch."

"Are you in pain?"

"Nope. Whatever's in this IV is doing the trick. In a few hours my ticker will be good as new."

"You give that ticker all the time it needs to get strong. And I swear, it's going to be daily walks and clean eating from now on. For both of us."

"Are the kids here?"

"Yes. Jason's got the girls at the hotel, but Lynette and Evan are right outside."

An anesthesiologist came in carrying an iPad. "Mr. Wiles I have to ask you a few questions, then I'll see you in the OR."

Susan squeezed his hand. "I'll see you afterwards. I love you."

"Love you too. I'm going to be fine."

Susan went back to the waiting area. "Lynette, they're taking him to surgery. It's going to be a few hours before we can see him."

"I'm going to run back to the hotel and check on the girls. Why don't you come with me?"

"I can't. I need to be close by."

"If you change your mind, call me. I won't be long." Lynette gave her a hug. "Dad's strong. He's going to be okay."

Susan sat down and flipped through a wrinkled *People* magazine with Michele Obama on the cover. The pages felt grimy and she wondered how many germy hands had touched it. She couldn't focus long enough to read more than a sentence here and there. Wes walked up behind her.

"Mrs. Wiles, didn't they show you where the surgery waiting room is? Come on, it'll be more comfortable. It could be a few hours."

"Thanks, Wes." She followed him into the elevator, noticing how he dragged his left leg behind him, making a rhythmic thud on the shiny floor with each step. She remembered the fire Cara's mom told her about when they spoke at the reception.

"You're shaking."

"I'm terrified that Mike is going to die."

"His cardiologist is the best in the state. Mike will be fine. I've got a few minutes before I need to get back." He pushed the button with his long, freckled fingers.

She hoped he was right. The elevator moved in slow motion. *Is this going to stop on every single floor?* The door opened on the next floor and Dr. Judith Potter entered carrying an armful of files. Susan smiled at her, then averted her eyes. How dumb. She probably didn't remember meeting her at the reception.

Judith Potter said, "You're Evan's mother, right? We met at the reception."

"Yes, I am. What a night that turned out to be."

"Poor Dr. Schmidt. Such a tragedy."

"I feel awful for his poor wife and son," said Susan. Gail losing her husband hit too close to her own heart at the moment.

"Yes, and the very idea of foul play. They questioned me about it this morning."

"You're saying he was drugged? Or poisoned?"

"Not necessarily, but the police did call me in and they asked if it looked to me like a heart attack."

"If he was poisoned, it had to have been someone at the party." For the first time in the past hour, Susan's thoughts veered away from Mike's health.

Wes said, "That's ridiculous. I can't imagine anyone from St. Agnes doing something so cruel. Besides, it happened right in front of a room full of witnesses, many of whom were doctors or med students. We all saw him keel over from a heart attack."

"If he was poisoned, or drugged, he could have ingested something hours before the party," said Judith.

"Who are you suspecting?" said Wes.

"If I were to speculate, I'd say his wife did it. I'll bet she caught on that her dear hubby was seeing someone on the side."

Susan was surprised by the personal comment. "How do you know that?"

"Two cell phones? Come on. We were both called in on a psych emergency last week to get a difficult patient under control. Afterwards, his phone rang. He pulled it out of his pocket, then mumbled something about it being *the other one*."

"The other one?"

"Yes. He pulled out a second phone from his other pocket and walked down the hall with it. On my way to the elevator, I saw him huddled in a corner and heard him say *I love you, too*."

"Maybe that was his wife, or his son." Susan had to admit her interest was piqued.

"I've heard him on the phone with his family before and, believe me, his tone was quite different. You know how when you're in love with someone you get that giddy baby voice? Well, that was him. And if it was an innocent call, why did he look so sheepish and take it out of earshot?"

His wife had access to the champagne. She could have even had a second, identical bottle and poisoned it ahead of time. Why kill him at the reception when she had access 24/7 to him?

Wes said, "This is our floor." Susan accidently bumped Judith Potter trying to get out, causing her to drop the armful of folders she was carrying.

"I'm so sorry. My husband was brought in here not too long ago and I've been shaking ever since. Here, let me pick those up," said Susan. Wes held the door.

"No, don't worry. I've got it," said Dr. Potter, scrambling to gather the papers and shove them back into folders.

Susan tried to stand up gracefully, but her back was aching. Wes offered her a hand.

"Again, I'm so sorry," said Susan, not finishing her sentence before the doors closed. Was what she'd just heard true, or just Judith Potter's interpretation? At the party, Dr. Schmidt and his wife seemed friendly enough toward each other. Now the son on the other hand…

She followed Wes down the corridor. "Wes, is there any reason she'd have been carrying files labeled with Dr. Schmidt's name?"

"Really? Is that how they were labeled?"

"Yes. What was in them do you think?"

"In this hospital, red folders are typically used for hard copies of research materials."

"Are you sure? Isn't everything electronic these days?"

"Most of it, but the consent forms, for example, have to be on paper. And it's easier, especially for the older doctors, to work off a hard copy if you're looking for data trends."

Did he really just refer to Judith Potter, who was middle aged by anyone's standards, as old? "And you're sure that's what the red folders are for?"

"Every research team I've been on since I started here has used that protocol."

"Did Dr. Potter and Dr. Schmidt ever work together? Like on a joint project?"

"I doubt it. They were both suspicious of each other and guarded their work."

"How do you know?"

"Word gets around. I'm wondering what she was doing with his files just now."

"Did you mention your suspicions to the police?"

"Yeah, I did. Here's the surgery waiting room. I've got to get back to work."

"Thanks, Wes. If you run into Evan, let him know where I am."

"Will do."

Wes was such a sweet boy. She was happy he and Evan were roommates. He walked away, dragging his left leg behind him. *Poor thing must have injured his leg in the fire.*

Susan settled into an overstuffed chair after grabbing a cup of cappuccino from the fancy machine by the door. Any more coffee and she'd never sleep that night. Not that she'd be able to anyway with Mike in the hospital. She leafed through the messages on her phone, trying to distract herself from worrying about Mike, but it wasn't working. Every few minutes she looked at the door, although she realized it was way too early to have news. Trying to escape the terror her mind was conjuring up, she focused her mind on the investigation. A murder mimicking a heart attack was less scary than Mike suffering from an actual one.

So, the police think Schmidt was poisoned. If Judith Potter is correct, Gail and Brian Schmidt both had motive. If she ever found out Mike was having an affair, she couldn't guarantee she wouldn't try to murder him! And the son, Brian. There was tension between him and his father, and teenage boys are notorious for their tempers. Not only had others mentioned it, she saw evidence of it herself. And what about Judith Potter? When did the feud between her and Dr. Schmidt start? Was she helping last night, or covering up her own nefarious deed?

She finished her drink, and played a game of *Words with Friends* on her phone. Then she scrolled through Facebook, crying at a post about a friend putting down her terminally ill dog that she'd owned for fifteen years. Only an hour had passed and it could be as much as five hours more. She went to WebMD on her phone and scrolled to the section 'complications from bypass surgery.'

Lynette came in. "What's wrong? Did you hear something?"

"Not yet. Look at this!" She showed Lynette the article on her phone. He could have permanent damage, or die in his sleep. I can't stop worrying. Why's it taking so long? I'll bet there were complications."

She took Susan's phone and turned it to off. "You heard them say it would take at least two or three hours. The success rate is something like 98%, remember the doctor said that?"

"I know. I have to keep reminding myself of that. It said online that he won't be able to travel for at least a month. I can't afford to stay at the hotel that long."

"I talked to Evan. He said you and Dad could stay with him. You'd have two doctors, Evan and Wes, right there if Dad needs them, and it's around the corner from here. Look how fast that ambulance came this morning."

"Can you stay for a while?"

"Only a few days. I wish I'd saved more vacation time. Jason has to be back at the university tomorrow so he's flying home with the girls tonight."

"Did they figure out if there was poison in the champagne? "

"Who said anything about poison?"

"Really, Lynette?"

"No, the champagne came back clean. They're searching the house now."

Lynette's phone vibrated. "Hello, Detective. No, I didn't notice him drinking coffee, just champagne. Really? Would that be enough to kill him? I'll ask. I'll call you back."

"Was that Detective Lowe?"

"Yes. They found traces of Visine in the coffee mug. She had in her notes that you saw Brian enter the living room, possibly from the kitchen and wanted me to ask you about it. Said your phone went to voicemail."

"I couldn't be sure where he came from. Is that what killed Dr. Schmidt? Visine?"

"It wasn't enough to kill him. They're searching for more evidence."

Susan went turned her phone back on and searched 'Visine as a poison.' *Often used as a prank...urban myth...causes extreme stomach upset, death.*

Lynette flipped through a magazine, then turned toward the door. "Mom, isn't that his doctor?"

"Mrs. Wiles?" Susan's legs shook as she stood up.

"Is he okay?"

"The surgery was a success. He's in ICU, but as soon as he comes out of the anesthesia you can see him."

"So he's out of the woods?" said Lynette.

"Barring complications, which I'm not expecting."

"Thanks, doctor. I could hug you!"

He took a step back. "I'm going to go check on him now."

Lynette said, "Mom, that's great news! I'll call Jason and let him know. Want to get lunch while we wait to see Dad?"

Susan hadn't noticed how hungry she was. "Sure, as long as we go no further than the cafeteria." Her head was throbbing and she hoped food might help.

Given the hour, the cafeteria line was short. Susan struggled over choosing a healthy salad or a burger with fries. She opted for the latter.

"Lynette, I've got to get Dad eating a heart healthy diet when he gets home or I might lose him."

"He was following the plan for a while after the original heart attack. I guess over time people let down their guard. That's typical."

"I'm going to order a heart-healthy cookbook on Amazon and try some new recipes."

"Why don't you go vegetarian? It's supposed to be good for you. I just saw a segment about it on one of those morning talk shows." She took a bite of her cheeseburger.

"No meat, no eggs, no cakes made with eggs…"

"That's not vegetarian. That's vegan. You don't have to go that far."

"I'll consider it. There's Boston Talmich." She waved for him to join them.

"I heard the surgery went smoothly," said Boston.

"I'm cautiously relieved. Now to keep it from ever happening again," said Susan.

He must have remembered Lynette was a detective. "Any news about the Schmidt investigation?" *Was she the only one who didn't know this was a potential homicide?*

"They found Visine in his coffee cup. They're investigating," announced Susan. Lynette glared at her.

Susan had a flashback to the night of the party. *Boston threw something into the fireplace. What was it?* "Do you think Judith Potter had anything to do with it?"

"Dr. Potter? I don't know."

"Wes and I bumped into her in the elevator. She dropped an armful of red folders with Dr. Schmidt's name on them."

"Red? Those are research folders."

"What if research was the motive? What if she killed him to steal his work?"

"I can't imagine her going to that extreme," said Boston. He slurped his fruit punch through a straw. "Then again, they had that awful argument the day before. Brian Schmidt is weird kid and the way he'd been acting lately..."

Lynette said, "I'm sure the police will figure it all out. Let's go check on Dad." She emptied their trays into the trash.

Boston said, "I'm heading up there, too. I volunteered to analyze some data for Dr. Potter, now that I'm no longer assisting Dr. Schmidt."

When they got out of the elevator, Susan sensed something wasn't right. She passed a police officer heading down the hall. Another officer stood guard in front of Dr. Schmidt's office.

Lynette showed her badge. "Everything okay, officer?"

"No. I was told to retrieve Dr. Schmidt's laptop and files but the laptop is gone, and the files are all over the floor. Someone beat me to it. I'm waiting for back up."

"Wasn't the door locked?" asked Lynette.

Boston said, "The psychology labs are back there. The offices all have access, and the interior doors don't lock, so if someone got in from another office, they could come right in."

Susan remembered the red folders. "Someone was very interested in getting their hands on his research."

"Or patient files," added Boston.

Chapter 5

Susan spent the night in a recliner next to Mike's bed. She fixated on the beeps coming from the machines, listening intently for a pause, holding her breath at the slightest variation in the pattern. The nurses were in and out of the ICU all night, monitoring his fluids and checking the incisions. She hadn't realized they'd cut a vein from Mike's leg to use in the operation until she saw the nurse change the dressing.

Doubting she'd slept at all, she was aware of the shift change. A new nurse introduced herself and reassured Susan that everything was on track.

"Later today, we'll get him out of bed. The sooner he gets up and about, the quicker he'll heal. Besides, we don't want blood clots to form."

Blood clots? Is that why he can't travel? When Lynette and Jason went to China to pick up Mia, Lynette mentioned they'd have to get up during the flight to avoid blood clots. She stared at Mike, watching his chest rise and fall…listening to the monitors…Her own heart jumped when he slowly opened his eyes.

"Can you hand me some water?" asked Mike. His voice was weak from exhaustion, and grainy from the tube that had been down his throat during the surgery. Susan carefully brought the straw to his lips.

It was difficult to maneuver around all the wires attached to his body. "I was so scared you were going to die."

"Nah. You're stuck with me. At least we get to extend our vacation. I'll have to call work and tell them."

"Lynette already took care of it. If someone has to wait a little longer to get their building permit, then so be it."

"I don't know how we can afford to stay in a hotel for a month."

That's what he's worried about? "Evan said we can stay with him and Wes."

The morning was punctuated with visits from various medical personnel.

The nurse came in. "We're going to get you out of bed later today, but first, the doctor ordered some tests. Transport will be here shortly."

Susan said, "Can I go with him?"

"I'm afraid not. You can wait here, or go get some lunch. It'll be a while. There's a Whole Foods around the corner."

Mike said, "Go eat. I'll be here. Besides, I should get some sleep before they try to get me out of bed. I feel like I've been run over by a truck."

Susan gave him a kiss, and set off to Whole Foods. Was building a health food store next to the hospital intentional, or had it been a coincidence? She felt rain drops, and remembered she'd left her umbrella at the Schmidt's the night of the reception. She hustled along, managing to mostly stay dry, keeping pace with the rhythm of the rain.

Whole Foods buzzed with activity. She stood in the take-out area, dizzy from the array of choices. She ended up with a mish mosh of items from the salad bar including lasagna, corn bread, and tabbouleh. Parched, she searched the shelves for a drink. *Why the heck don't they sell diet soda? I can't stand those Stevia sweetened drinks.*

She found a table in the café area. Valerie, the detective's mother, came up behind her.

"Hey, I thought you were going back to New York. Want company?"

"I'd love company. The plan was to head home, but unfortunately we've had a delay. Mike had…" She couldn't get the words out.

"Are you okay? What happened to Mike?"

"He had, he had um…, he had a heart attack yesterday. They did a bypass."

"Oh my goodness! Is he okay?"

"Right now he is, but who knows what might happen. I was reading online and there are all sorts of possible complications."

"Reading on line? You need to listen to what his doctors say, not some internet mumbo jumbo."

"I should have kept him on track with his eating and exercise. I feel like if I'd nagged him more after the last time, this wouldn't have happened." *Who was she kidding? She couldn't even keep herself on track.*

"He's a grown man and you ain't his mother. You can't make someone else's choices for them. We're all the boss of our own lives."

"I guess you're right, but I wish I'd encouraged him to keep taking walks together after dinner."

"It ain't easy. I was just at the hospital myself visiting my own cardiologist. My blood pressure is way up there and they haven't gotten my medication dosage right. They tell me to lose weight and cut out salt. Easy for them to say." She took a spoonful of her soup, then picked up the salt shaker.

Susan made a face as she swallowed the poor excuse for soda. "How's your daughter doing with the case?"

"Well, she refuses to discuss it with me, but I can't help if I overhear her talking about it. She was on the phone yesterday when I dropped off Elijah and I heard her say they found traces of Visine in his orange juice, and in the water cooler he had in his office."

"So it wasn't just in the coffee cup. It had to be someone who had access to his home and office. That could be his wife, his son...or someone he worked with who was also at the reception." She crumbled the corn bread pulling it apart from the wrapper. "There's a doctor, Judith Potter, who was overheard arguing with Dr. Schmidt. I heard there was bad blood between them. She was at the reception, *and* her office connects to the shared psychology lab at the hospital."

"Any hard evidence, or just speculation?"

You can tell she's been around law enforcement, or else she watches all the lawyer shows like I do. "I saw her with a handful of Dr. Schmidt's research folders."

"Really?"

"Yeah, and Dr. Schmidt's laptop was stolen, and his office files ransacked. She had access to his office."

"I hope Jazmin's nailing her."

A tall blonde carrying a box of books was setting up a display on a table in the front of the café area. She put a cloth over the table and pulled a plastic picture frame from her bag.

Susan said, "What's going on? She's unpacking a stack of books." She pushed her bifocals up. "*The Lazy Vegetarian.*"

"I saw a sign up front. She's some author who wrote a cookbook. I guess we're about to find out cause I ain't done with my lunch and this big old butt ain't leaving this seat."

The woman neatly arranged her books and business cards on the table while little by little, the café filled up. Susan scanned the room for vegetarians. *I don't see any skinny, bare-faced, bell bottom clad hippies.* Instead, she saw men and women in white coats and scrubs, a couple of soccer moms, backpack-clad students, and white-haired retirees.

The author spoke. "Welcome, one and all. I'm Lacey Daniels and I want to introduce my new book, *The Lazy Vegetarian*. Few would disagree that a vegetarian diet is optimal for both health and moral reasons. The biggest obstacle as I see it is the inconvenience of preparing vegetarian meals from scratch. My book brings the benefits of vegetarian eating to the masses."

Susan's ears perked up. How fateful that this author was here just when she was worried about creating healthy menus for Mike and herself.

"Yeah, right. I ain't eating salad when Jazzy offers to take me to dinner at Outback. And who has the kind of money to buy all those organic fruits and vegetables?"

Then Lacey held up her book. "Let me demonstrate." She opened a can of black beans and threw a bag of microwavable rice into the portable microwave. Then she opened a can of diced, chunky tomatoes seasoned with chilies and drained off the water. "These are nonperishable items you can keep on hand in your pantry." The microwave beeped. She took the rice out and dumped it into a bowl. Then she mixed the tomatoes with the black beans and threw it into the microwave for a minute and a half. "Now, you can use a bit of soft cheese or shredded Mexican blend if you like." She put the cheese on the rice and poured the hot black beans with tomatoes on top. "Voila!"

Susan whispered, "That doesn't look half bad."

"I'm skeptical," said Valerie.

Lacey passed around samples. "You can make this meal for pennies a serving."

Susan took a bite. "This is really good."

Valerie tried a spoonful. "Jazzy could take this for lunch and reheat it in the microwave at the station."

The author said, "I'll be demonstrating recipes here all week long if you'd like to learn more, and I'm giving a series of talks at the St. Agnes Hospital cafeteria. There are schedules up front. Meanwhile, I'll be signing books for the next half an hour."

Susan said, "I'm going to buy one."

Valerie picked one up off the table and flipped through it, then got in line behind her.

When she got to Lacey Daniels, she said, "Can I use my AARP discount?"

"Of course. Who should I sign it for?"

"For Susan and Mike. That's me and my husband."

"Susan and Mike. My email and website are listed in back. Don't hesitate to contact me if you have questions."

Chapter 6

The next day, Mike had moved out of ICU and into a regular room. Susan poured him a cup of water and held the straw to his cracked lips. He tried to sit up.

A male nurse came in, checked his pulse, and checked the monitors. "Heart rate's good. Fluid levels look good, no fever." He looked at the incision on Mike's chest. "How's your pain on a scale of one to ten?"

"Twelve. The cut on my thigh hurts just as bad. And it itches."

"Every day will be better. I'll bring you some Tylenol."

"Tylenol? Why not baby Aspirin? You've got nothing stronger?"

The nurse ignored the comment. "Let's get you up."

"Up? As in out of bed? You're kidding, right?"

He raised the bed back and lowered the side rail. "Mrs. Wiles, your job is to push the IV pole, got it?" He slipped gripper socks on Mike's feet.

"Got it." She felt Mike's pain as he winced and struggled to stand.

"Mr. Wiles, if you feel dizzy let me know. It's not a race. We can take all the time you need." He supported Mike, holding him under his armpits. They headed out the door.

Susan pushed the IV pole alongside them. Then she realized to her horror that Mike's backside was uncovered. With one hand pushing the pole, she held the gown together with the other.

"Easy does it, Mr. Wiles. You'll be out there running marathons in no time."

Susan's back was beginning to ache as she stooped over to hold the hospital gown in one hand while pushing the pole. *I'm the one who's going to need Tylenol.*

"You've got to get up and walk as much as you can. It'll speed up your recovery," said the nurse.

Susan said, "What if he has another heart attack while we're out walking? What do I do if I have to leave the house to get groceries?"

"By the time he leaves here, you won't have to babysit him. We'll set him up with a monitor to wear at home. Anything abnormal and the doctor will be alerted."

"What if the ambulance doesn't get there in time?"

"We don't expect any ambulance rides. He's being closely watched, and if need be, the doctor can insert a portable defibrillator."

"More surgery?"

"Don't put the cart before the horse. We expect a full, uncomplicated recovery."

Two pretty young nursing students came down the hall. Susan gripped Mike's gown more tightly, trailing behind him like an appendage.

"You okay there, Mrs. Wiles?"

"Oh, yeah. Just fine."

"Mr. Wiles, you're doing great. Feeling okay?"

"Feeling a little winded."

"We'll turn around when we get to the nurse's station. Easy does it."

No fewer than half a dozen patients and nurses stared at her awkward effort to protect her husband's modesty as they headed back to Mike's room.

"There. Good job. Let's get you back into bed."

While the nurse got Mike situated, Susan plopped into the chair next to the bed. She hadn't slept much at all and her head hurt. Her body had been in a constant state of alert since they brought Mike in. She didn't know how much more she could take. When would she relax and stop thinking he was going to die at any second?

After the nurse left, Mike said, "I'll be going home in a few days." He tried to reach the water on the night table. Susan got up and handed it to him.

"Mike, don't push it. You have to rest and let your body heal. You'll go home when your body feels strong enough and the doctors give the okay. Meanwhile, you've got TV, three meals a day, nurses waiting on you hand and foot…" She picked up a pamphlet from the bedside table. "What's this?"

"A dietician came by. Part of my cardiac rehab team."

"What'd she tell you?"

"She gave me some diet."

Susan skimmed over it. "Mostly fruits, vegetables, whole grains, and chicken. It does allow for a small portion of lean steak and a beer now and then." She hadn't forgotten what Lynette mentioned about going vegetarian, wondering if it'd be healthier for them both.

"It's still a diet."

Ignoring the comment, she continued. "I picked up this book yesterday. *The Lazy Vegetarian*, by Lacey Daniels. I heard her presentation at Whole Foods." She immediately caught the protest in Mike's narrowing eyes.

Mike objected. "I never agreed to tofu and lettuce."

"We can try it out and see how we do. She did a cooking demo yesterday at Whole Foods. Rice and beans. It was tasty and took minutes to make."

"You sound like an infomercial."

Lynette walked in. "How are you feeling, Dad? My flight is today. Wish I could stay longer."

Mike said, "I'm already feeling much better."

"He went for a walk down the hall a little while ago."

"Good, Dad. But what if you have a set back and you and Mom need help?"

"We'll be staying with two doctors, your brother and his roommate, and the hospital is around the corner."

Susan added, "Wes is even a cardiology resident."

Lynette's phone vibrated. "Hey, Jazmin. Really? You have him in for questioning? Great. I'm heading home today but I appreciate being included."

Susan said, "Did they find the killer?"

"The son, Brian. They picked him up for questioning. They found bottles of Visine stashed under his mattress and in his backpack."

Susan was surprised Lynette so freely volunteered the information. Perhaps being out of her jurisdiction, the same code of ethics didn't apply. "So he killed his own father?"

If he'd given him multiple doses, maybe."

"Why?"

"That's what I'd like to know," said Lynette. "Anyway, I need to get to the airport. I spoke to Jason this morning and Annalise had talked him into eating leftover pizza washed down with chocolate banana smoothies for breakfast. "

"Technically it's a balanced meal," said Susan. "Protein from the milk and cheese, the sauce is a vegetable, and the banana…"

"Seriously, Mom? I appreciate you sticking up for Annalise, but when her teacher calls Jason to pick her up because she has a stomachache, it won't be funny. Jason has a full schedule of classes this semester."

"Have a safe trip," said Mike.

"Don't let Mom fix your meals!" Lynette leaned over and gave her father a kiss. "You listen to your doctor and follow instructions so you can get home to us soon."

Susan looked out the window. "It's raining like the dickens. I hope your flight will be on time. Oh, and I left my umbrella at Dr. Schmidt's house the night of the reception. Maybe I should swing by."

"Mom, stop. I know you want to stop by there to probe the poor widow about murder suspects. Stay out of it. Dad needs you."

Lynette gave her a kiss on the cheek and closed the door behind her.

"I wish I could fly home today, too." Mike's voice was scratchy and weak.

"The doctor says you can't fly for several weeks. It'll give us a chance to visit with Evan and get to know Cara better. We can FaceTime the girls every night."

The door swung open. "Knock, knock. Mr. Wiles, I'm taking you down to the physical therapy suite."

Susan said, "Already? He's barely been out of bed."

"It's just an orientation to the program his therapist is prescribing. Don't worry, ma'am. They know what they're doing."

She found it hard to trust the authority of this boy who looked no older than the teenage neighbor who fed Meow Mix to Ludwig and Johann when she and Mike were out of town. She followed them as far as the elevator. "When will he be back in his room?"

"Give him a couple of hours," said the orderly.

With time to kill, Susan considered picking up some food and swinging by the Schmidt home. If she didn't distract herself, she'd go crazy. The last thing poor Mrs. Schmidt needed to think about right now was cooking and besides, she needed that umbrella.

After running into Whole Foods to pick up a container of butternut squash soup and a veggie lasagna, she hailed a cab, took out her phone, and pulled up the Schmidt's address. The kids had taught her how to use Uber, which was much cheaper than a taxi, but she didn't have the patience right now to mess with it.

"Where to, ma'am?"

"Here's the address." She showed the driver her phone.

During the ride, she second guessed herself about leaving the hospital. *Sit in Mike's empty hospital room, or do a good deed? It's not like Mike isn't surrounded by doctors if he has a problem.*

She imagined herself in Gail Schmidt's shoes and it hit too close to home. How must Gail feel living in that house, seeing her husband's clothes in the closet, his coffee mug on the counter? Her heart ached thinking about the emptiness she must be feeling. *A bit of company and some hot food might help a little. What would help more? Nailing her husband's killer.*

When she arrived at the Schmidt's, it was still raining. *See, I do need that umbrella.* The doorbell chimes could be heard from the stoop.

Gail Schmidt wore no makeup and her cheeks were damp with tears. "Yes?"

"Mrs. Schmidt, I'm so sorry for your loss. I don't know if you remember me, Susan Wiles. My son studied with your husband and we were at the reception the night…that night."

"Oh, yes." She looked at the armload of food and stood in the doorway still for a few minutes before saying, "Come on in." She stuffed a tissue into the pocket of her jeans.

"I'm sure cooking is the last thing on your mind right now so I brought something for you and your son. Want me to put it in the fridge?"

Gail took the food from Susan's arms. "No, I've got it." She stood still as if waiting for Susan to turn around and say goodbye.

"I left my umbrella here the other night." She searched through the umbrella stand in the foyer. "Here it is."

"Is Brian home?"

"Brian? Not at the moment."

She remembered he was at the station being questioned. "I'll bet he's taking this hard." She made her way into the living room and sat on the sofa. Gail followed her.

"I'm not sure what he thinks. He and his father weren't on good terms lately."

"It was still his father. I'll bet he feels awful having left things unresolved."

"It's that Judith who should feel awful. Always on Neil's case, criticizing his research…I can't help wondering…"

"Wondering what?" Susan's ears froze in anticipation of a juicy clue.

Gail's phone buzzed. "I have to take this. It's the funeral home."

Gail went into the kitchen with her phone. She heard Gail say something about *not being welcomed. The fireplace!* Susan thought about the crumpled paper she saw Boston toss in there and couldn't resist. She walked over and saw it, charred, but lying right in plain sight behind the burnt log.

She carefully picked it up and shook off the ashes. It was somewhat burnt on the edges, but she could still read part of it. *922…I can't read the last number.*

Avenue. This is someone's address. Why did he throw it away and whose address is it?

Gail returned to the living room. Susan stuffed the note in her jacket pocket. "Is everything okay? Can I do anything for you?"

"No, it's nothing. If you'll excuse me, I have arrangements to make. The funeral is day after tomorrow."

They're already releasing the body? They must have found what they are looking for...or not. Susan gathered the umbrella and said, "Again, I'm sorry for what you and your son are going through. I know Evan thought highly of him."

Gail pushed the door closed and it nearly grazed Susan's behind as she left. *Now, where's that Uber app?* She successfully arranged a ride and waited at the curb. Brian Schmidt screeched into the driveway and he stormed up the stoop, slamming the front door behind him. Hadn't he been picked up for questioning? He wasn't carrying a backpack...

The rain, which had been on again off again all morning, was back on. She popped open the umbrella and hoped her ride would hurry up. Around the corner, she spotted a blue Grand Marquis parked at the edge of the property. The windows were tinted and she couldn't be sure whether or not it was occupied. She edged closer. Suddenly, the car started and as quickly as an old workhouse could move, it pulled out from the curb and sped away.

Challenging her imagination, she invented scenarios. Maybe Gail was seeing someone who got jealous and killed her hubby. Perhaps the two of them plotted the murder together and when he saw Susan pull up, he didn't want to chance a witness seeing him go in. She couldn't even be sure whether it was a man or a woman driving the car. For all she knew, someone pulled over to check an address. *I have to stop connecting the dots before I'm sure there are dots to connect.* At least it was taking her mind off the possibility of becoming a widow. Her ride arrived.

She sat in back and dozed off and on until she was dropped off at the hospital. She hoped Mike hadn't been wondering where she was.

In the lobby, she ran into Judith Potter. Wrestling to close the wet umbrella, she said, "You really stepped up to the plate when Neil Schmidt collapsed."

"I wish I could have done more. We didn't always see eye to eye professionally, but Neil will be missed. I hope Gail never finds out about the other woman."

"I'm sure it would break her heart."

"Let's hope sleeping dogs are left alone. I need to hurry." She disappeared around the corner.

Susan pressed the elevator button. When the door opened, she came face to face with Valerie Lowe.

"Valerie, is everything okay?"

"Yeah. Had a follow up with my doctor, that's all. I mentioned the vegetarian thing and that we'd seen that presentation over at Whole Foods. He thought it was an excellent idea. That author's giving lunch time lectures in the cafeteria all this week. I was considering heading down there, then talked myself out of it."

Susan said, "Let's go. Let me check on Mike, then meet you down there. I am a bit hungry." She felt shaky. With all that was going on, she was sorely neglecting her own type 2 diabetes.

When she got to Mike's room, he was fast asleep, the monitors humming contently. She whispered in his ear, "I'm going to grab a quick lunch. I'll be right downstairs." She kissed his cheek and went down to the cafeteria where Valerie was already in line.

Susan took a spinach wrap with a side of macaroni and cheese. "I heard they picked up Neil Schmidt's son for questioning. They found Visine in his backpack."

"I overheard Jazzy talking to her colleague when I stopped by to pick up Elijah's show-and-tell model that he left on the kitchen table. I heard her say the autopsy showed he didn't die from the Visine."

"But I was just with the wife, and she says the funeral is day after tomorrow. They must have released the body."

"Maybe they got whatever samples they need, or didn't find anything at all. Who knows, could have actually been a heart attack, right?"

"I suppose."

"Except," Valerie lowered her voice. "I heard Jazzy say they had to look for another cause of death. Didn't sound like it happened naturally to me."

"If it wasn't the Visine, and the champagne was clean, what was it?"

"They said he never had heart problems in the past."

"Guess what? I saw a blue car staking out the Schmidt home when I went to fetch my umbrella. It peeled off when it noticed I was watching it. And Judith Potter thinks Neil Schmidt was having an affair."

"So the wife or the mistress?"

"Could be." She remembered the note. "Look, I found this in the fireplace. I saw Boston Talmich, a psych resident, toss it into the fireplace the night of the reception. It looks like an address."

"What's he got to do with this?"

"No idea, but he wanted it destroyed. He worked with Dr. Schmidt, and maybe Judith Potter too. Contact info for the mistress?"

"To blackmail Schmidt over the affair and wreck his credibility?"

"Not sure if that would even matter professionally. Oh, looks like Lacey Daniels is starting her lecture. Come on, let's find a seat."

They sat at a small table in a partitioned area of the cafeteria. Lacey Daniels passed around samples of chick-pea quesadillas, then began talking about the correlation between a high fat diet and heart disease. Valerie whispered, "Like that's something we didn't know?"

Lacey continued, "A little fat is necessary so our bodies can absorb certain vitamins and keep us satiated so we won't be tempted to overdo it on the wrong types of foods. I give my hospital patients guidelines. Most have a false assumption they can't ever eat real butter or full fat dairy products…"

When Lacey finished, Susan asked her for advice about Mike. "Do you work directly with the cardiac patients at the hospital?"

"I did, but now I mostly supervise. I'd be glad to speak to your husband, though all the dieticians there are terrific."

"Have you been working there long?"

"A few years. I was pulled in to work with one of the psychiatrists on a study back a few years ago, and when a position opened up, I accepted."

"Psychiatry?"

"Yeah. How food affects brain development …looking at the difference nutrition makes in expressing genetic traits. We worked with twin studies mostly."

"So you must have known Dr. Schmidt."

"Neil Schmidt? Yes, I consulted for him. Poor man. I was shocked when I heard the news."

"And Judith Potter?"

"I'd run into her a few times, but just last week she approached me at the hospital. She needed some help with a case she was working on. We were supposed to meet the day after Neil died but she had to go to the police station for an interview and I've been busy promoting my book." Lacey looked at her watch. "I have a meeting to get to. My publicist has some things she wants to go over with me. Here's my card if you have any questions regarding your husband."

Chapter 7

"Mike, no! I'm coming, where are you?" Susan woke with a start. She was having a dream that Mike had fallen off a bridge into a violent river. She jumped in after him, swimming furiously, but she couldn't reach him. When she opened her eyes, she'd fallen off Evan's couch to the floor. Thank goodness he had carpeting.

"Mom, are you okay? I heard you screaming. What are you doing on the floor?"

"I'm fine. I was having a bad dream, that's all." He held out his hand and helped her up.

Yesterday, Evan helped her move their things from the hotel to his apartment. The four story apartment overlooked Forest Park and was around the corner from both the med school and St. Agnes. Couldn't ask for a more convenient location, and St. Louis was much more affordable than many other cities Evan and Cara had contemplated when deciding where they wanted to do their residencies.

"Mom, I've got to get to the hospital, but there are eggs in the fridge and bread in the freezer. I'm going to drop by and see Dad before work. Dr. Schmidt's funeral is this afternoon. I'll come by to change after lunch."

"I'll probably see you at the hospital. I'm going with you to the funeral."

"You don't have to. You barely knew him."

"I want to show support for his wife. Besides, it's not like my schedule is particularly full. Dad has cardiac rehab most of the afternoon."

After Evan left, Susan poured herself a cup of coffee and defrosted a few slices of bread. The fridge was mostly bare, with half a carton of orange juice, some protein shakes, and a couple of apples. She heard the key in the door. Evan's roommate came in wearing running shorts and holding a water bottle.

"Hi, Wes."

"Hope you slept well."

"Yes, I did. Thanks for sharing your apartment while we're in town."

"With the hours I spend at the hospital, I'm only here to sleep or grab a meal. As a matter of fact, you and your husband are welcome to use my room. The couch can't be very comfortable and it certainly isn't big enough for two. He's going to be pretty sore from the surgery for a while and it will be hard enough to get comfortable."

"Are you sure?"

"Like I said, I'm hardly here. If I have time off, I spend it over at my girlfriend's place."

"I can't wait to have Mike home. Do you think he'll be okay from now on? I can't stop worrying about him."

"If he follows his instructions, I don't see him having complications."

"Thanks, Wes. By the way, are you going to the funeral this afternoon?"

"Yes. The school was gracious enough to give us time off to attend. It's sure to be a packed house."

After Wes left, Susan unpacked Mike's things and moved her clothes to Wes's room. She sat down to read, and couldn't keep her eyes open. Mittens scratched at the door, waking her up in time to get ready for the funeral.

Evan stopped at home to change. They picked up Cara and drove to the service.

"Cara, you must be thrilled that you get to stay here in St. Louis. You grew up here, right?"

"I did. The pediatrics department is excellent here and I've already worked with some of the doctors."

"I'm happy you and Evan will be together. I'll bet your parents are, too. Are you moving into Evan's place after graduation?"

Evan gave her a stern look. "Why are you interrogating my girlfriend?"

Girlfriend sounds trite at his age. He should be calling her his fiancée.

"It's fine," said Cara. "Evan and I talked about finding a new place together. One with a washer and dryer. I'm tired of hauling laundry down to the basement."

The brick synagogue in University City was nestled into a residential area alongside Delmar Blvd. It looked like the other brick places they passed, except for the glass, a-framed front entrance. They pulled around back, finding the last available parking space. At the door, Evan was handed a yarmulke which he placed clumsily on his head.

Susan hadn't been to a Jewish service in many years and was struck by the contrast to the elaborate Catholic funeral she'd attended last month back in Westbrook. The inside of the temple was clean and simple, like Danish furniture. No stained glass or padded pews for kneeling. She and Evan sat with Cara near the back behind Boston, Wes, and Judith Potter. At first, Susan was surprised to see Lacey Daniels walk in and take a seat next to Judith Potter. Then she remembered Lacey saying she'd consulted on some psychology research, which is how she wound up with a position at St. Agnes.

In the front row, Gail Schmidt was sobbing next to her son, Brian. To her other side were several people she assumed were relatives. The rabbi took the podium and began the service.

"Neil Schmidt was a fine man, loved by his family and friends. He's at peace, now." The cantor sang, and the congregation prayed. Gail Schmidt, mascara running like black tar, took the podium next to her son.

"The day I married Neil was one of the happiest days of my life, along with the day our son was born. Neil was a fine husband, with a way of making me feel special, even after twenty years of marriage. He'd come home with flowers or surprise me with weekend get-aways." She broke down, and Brian put his arm around her, taking the microphone.

"My father taught me to bowl when I was in second grade. His big hands guided my arm and he taught me just how low to stoop before I released the ball and it went charging down the alley crashing the pins, causing them to collapse. He was someone to look up to. A winner no matter who he was up against."

Susan heard nothing but sincerity as she watched his quivering lower lip. Did he really try to kill his father with Visine, or was it a half-hearted expression of teenage anger?

The service was truly a tribute to Neil Schmidt. Friends and colleagues then took turns relaying stories of what a warm and generous man Neil had been.

In the middle of the service, Susan felt a tickle in her throat. She worked to stifle a cough but the more she worried about making noise, the drier her throat became. Evan whispered, "I saw a water fountain when we came in."

The dean of the medical school ran through Neil's curriculum vitae, emphasizing the research, grants, and awards he'd won over the years.

"Dr. Neil Schmidt presented his research on nature vs. nurture at conferences around the globe. The world is a better place for the knowledge he left behind."

Now the coughing was hard to control. Susan wrapped her scarf around her mouth, trying to muffle it. She searched her purse for a sucking candy. At the bottom, covered in tissue lint, she found an old peppermint from the last time they ate at a steakhouse back in New York. She untwisted the cellophane wrapper, but the sticky candy was stubborn.

She worked frantically, the cough getting more insistent. The congregation became abruptly silent in prayer and the wrapper crinkled like crackling thunder in a night sky. Boston and Judith turned around and gave her dirty looks.

"Mom, go get a drink," whispered Evan.

Thankfully, Neil Schmidt's brother was up there telling stories about when he and Neil were kids. The metal folding chair creaked as she got up. More dirty looks.

"Let's have a moment of silence as we remember the joy Neil brought to our lives." His brother bowed his head and the congregation followed suit.

Darn it. He couldn't have told some funny story about his brother, making the congregation laugh. No. More solemn silence.

She tried to be discreet, in spite of sticking her butt in the faces of the entire row on her way to the aisle. With every stumble and 'excuse me' she felt more mortified. If only she'd stuck to Weight Watchers, this would have been a lot easier.

When she finally made it out the back door, sweating like she'd been in a steam room, she gulped water, waited to be sure the coughing had subsided, and took a few deep breaths. Then, she noticed a large, middle-aged man sobbing near the rest room. At least it appeared to be a man. He or she was wearing a long tweed coat and had a scarf pulled around his or her face. The coat collar muffled wet sobs. She contemplated offering condolences, but was too late, the person disappeared out the front door.

Through the door, she saw a dark blue sedan double parked in front of a BMW. As it zipped away with the unknown person now inside, she remembered where she'd seen it. It was the Grand Marquis that had been parked outside the Schmidt home when she'd dropped off food for Gail. *Who was that person and why was he sneaking around instead of joining the congregation?* She wished she'd have been able to catch the license number.

The cantor was singing, and she decided this might be a good time to re-enter. When they saw her coming, the whole row stood to let her pass through.

"You okay, Mom?"

She wasn't sure if there was a hint of annoyance in Evan's question, or if her embarrassment over her clumsy exit had made her oversensitive. "I'm fine."

When the service ended, the rabbi announced that the Schmidt family had invited everyone to come back to their house and that they'd be sitting Shiva starting tomorrow.

When they arrived at the house, Susan overheard a conversation between Gail and her son.

"He was cheating on you. Don't you care?"

"It's not that. It's not what you think. Don't go ruining your father's good name."

Susan flushed when Gail came around the corner, barking. "Can I get you something?"

"No, I…was just coming in for a cup of water. My throat's got a tickle." *Did Gail just roll her eyes at me?*

"There's cold water through the fridge door." Gail handed her a glass. "Now if you'll excuse me."

Brian leaned on the counter, finishing a can of Red Bull.

"I hope I didn't intrude. You seem upset. Not that you wouldn't be with your father and everything." She felt the walls of the corner she'd painted herself into choking her.

"Mom thinks Dad was some sort of hero. Truth is he was making a fool out of her. Out of both of us till I caught on."

"What do you mean? I just met them both, but at the reception on Match Day they looked happy together."

"Dad was out every Thursday night. Told Mom he was bowling with a team from the med school."

"So?"

"One night I went into the basement to look for something and I saw his bowling ball bag sitting there smack in the middle of the old pool table."

"Maybe he used the ones at the alley. That's what Mike and I, my husband, do when we go bowling."

"No. He took me bowling a lot when I was a kid. Dad took bowling seriously and had a custom-made ball. He broke his thumb when he was younger and had the thumb hole drilled to fit it."

"That still doesn't prove…"

"Yeah, well, the next week I followed him. Out to Clayton. Saw him pull up in front of this cutesy brick place. He practically pranced up to the door."

"Do you know who it was he was seeing?"

"No, but I stayed long enough to see whoever it was pull down the window shade. I heard him come home, must have been around 1 a.m., after Mom was asleep."

"Was there a big, blue Grand Marquis in the driveway?"

"Yeah. How do you know?"

"I saw it parked across the street the day I came over to fetch my umbrella. And, I saw it earlier today at the synagogue."

"So you know I'm right."

"Looks like your suspicions have merit, but why bring it up? Your mother is already suffering. What good does it do, adding salt to the wound?"

"I think whoever Dad was seeing may have poisoned him."

"Why?"

"Last Thursday, Dad stayed home. I heard his end of a phone conversation out on the back porch. He was breaking it off. He said he had commitments to keep and was arguing, but the woman wasn't taking no for an answer."

"Did you tell the police?"

"Not without my Mom's blessing. Like you said, she's hurting enough. Besides, I have no proof of anything."

"Do you have access to your dad's phone?"

"I guess it's still here somewhere, maybe in his office or the bedroom."

"If we find it, I'm sure the police could pull up records of the calls."

Brian peeked into the living room. "They're all busy sobbing out there. Come on." He led her past the bathroom she'd used the other night and up the staircase. "In here."

Susan found herself in a small office with a heavy wood desk, bookshelves, and a Tiffany-style floor lamp. "Can I start here?"

"Yeah. Check the desk. I'll look under this pile next to the recliner."

Susan methodically went through the desk, drawer by drawer. The bottom drawer was locked. "Do you know where he might have a key?"

"Check under the blotter."

Susan lifted the leather desk blotter and it was almost too easy. A small gold key was in plain sight. She inserted it into the lock and the file drawer was free. She rifled through to see if she could find the phone, or a secret burner phone. Then she noticed the files. They were red like the ones Judith Potter had dropped. The folders were neatly labeled and arranged chronologically. She pulled one out. *Permission to participate in research study. Records of visits and a personality checklist…*

"Did you find it?"

"Uh, no. Not in here." She heard footsteps.

"Brian, are you up here? Your uncle is leaving. He wants to say goodbye."

"Shh." Brian turned off the light and opened the door. "I'll be right down, Mom."

Susan followed Brian down the stairs and worked her way back to the living room, where Judith Potter and Boston Talmich were engaged in a private conversation. She moved closer trying to decipher the whispering.

She heard Boston say, "Yeah, it was impulsive. I'm going to do it this time. Text me the address."

Judith answered, "It'll be a shock, but it's about time the truth came out and it may be beneficial to both of you." Then she took a step back and nearly bumped into Susan.

"Clumsy me," said Susan. I was just trying to make my way closer to the lovely fire."

Judith took a deep breath and smiled. "You should stay warm and get that nasty cough taken care of. Is Evan here with you?"

"He was but he had to go back to school. I'll Uber back to his place afterwards."

"I can drop you back if you'd like," said Boston. "Evan lives in my building."

Susan had another drink, scarfed down a few rugalach, and said goodbye to Gail.

"I'm ready when you are."

Boston led her to a gray Toyota and like a true gentleman, opened the door for her. She'd imagined doctors driving fancier cars, but on the way home, Boston told her how he and his recently graduated friends were consumed with paying off their med school debt as quickly as possible.

"It's a 2011, but she runs like a kitten. It's all about maintenance."

"Do you think you'll wind up staying here in St. Louis? When you finish your residency, I mean."

"Depends. If they offer me an attending position, it would be hard to turn down. I learned a lot from Doctor Schmidt and now I'm learning a lot working with Dr. Potter."

"Dr. Schmidt did research as well as teach, right?" She tried to sound casual now, but wasn't sure she'd pulled it off.

"Yeah, he was into research."

"What was his focus?"

"You heard the dean at the service. Twin studies, mostly. Nature vs. Nurture. The same old same old."

"Do you think his work will continue, now that he's you know, deceased?"

"Had to be ethical first and foremost," Boston mumbled under his breath.

"What?"

"Nothing. Yes, I'll bet his work lives on. Here we are."

Evan and Boston lived around the corner from the med school/hospital complex. The four-story building sat on the corner of a shaded street across from Forest Park, around the bend from the hospital and med school complex, and down the road from Whole Foods. She rode up the elevator with Boston, getting out on the third floor, fumbling for the key Evan gave her.

"If you need anything, I'm right upstairs in 402."

"Thanks for bringing me back. I'm just going to take a nap, I'm worn out."

She opened the door, careful to heed Evan's warning about not letting the cat out. She sensed the vague smell of a litter box. She turned on the lights. To the right was a galley-style kitchen with an island that opened into the dining area. Evan had constructed a tall cat tree and Mittens was resting on the top tier. She plopped her purse on the table, took off her coat, and said hello to the tuxedo cat. She was greeted with a hiss. *Guess she's protecting her territory.*

Susan's suitcase was on the floor in Wes's room, where the bed sported fluffy pillows and a denim comforter. It was neater and homier than she'd expected. Last time she'd visited, Evan's room was cluttered with clothing and books lying everywhere. Wes left a note on the bed. *I'll be staying at my girlfriend's apartment. Make yourself at home.*

She unzipped the suitcase and changed into stretchy pants and a long sleeve t-shirt. They weren't expecting to stay more than a few days, and she'd already put away Mike's things. She opened the closet looking for a place to hang the one good dress she'd packed. Afterwards, she opened the dresser drawers. The top and adjacent one were each half empty so she took the liberty of consolidating the items to free up a space.

She threw away an empty pack of gum and a crumpled fast food receipt. Then she found a wrinkled photograph of two boys and a red-haired woman, who Susan assumed was a younger version of Wes's mother. The boys were nearly identical, both resembled a younger Wes. *This must be the boy who died in the fire.* She jumped when she heard the apartment door open, then quickly grabbed Mike's boot and slid behind the door, heart pounding.

"Mom, I'm home."

She relaxed when she heard Evan's voice. Throwing down the boot, she shut the door behind her. "I thought you had to work?"

"I got out early. I felt guilty about not getting you settled."

"Boston delivered me right to your door. He's quite a gentleman. And Wes was awfully considerate, giving up his room like that."

"He practically lives over at Bethany's place anyway."

"I didn't know Wes had a brother. I thought he was an only child."

"That's news to me."

"I found a photo in his dresser drawer…"

"Mom, are you snooping already?"

"No, I was just making space to unpack a few things."

"He was nice enough to offer you and Dad his room. The least you can do is respect his privacy."

"Do you think they'll get married? When's a good time for you all—med students, I mean—to get married? Between med school and residency?"

"Mom, stop."

"I'm just saying, like with you and Cara, the next five years are going to be very busy, right? And I'm sure Cara wants a family. Didn't she just turn twenty-nine?"

"I'm going to the gym. Help yourself to whatever food you can find."

Chapter 8

Susan dreamt she was in a wind tunnel, reaching for Mike's hand. The harder she tried to reach him, the further away he blew. She woke, sweating through her nightgown, to the sound of the blinds jingling. Mittens batted at the slats and sunlight peeked through the window. *It's more stressful to sleep than to be awake these days.*

"Mittens, come here, baby." Mittens looked like a tiger ready to pounce. She leapt onto the bed, over Susan's legs, and out the bedroom door. She craved kitty cuddles from Johann and Ludwig back home. The aroma of fresh coffee lured her out of bed. After changing out of the damp nightgown, she went into the kitchen where Evan was making breakfast.

"I'm making scrambled eggs. Want some?" Evan poured himself a cup of coffee. Mittens was curled on top of the cat tree. Hard to believe she'd been darting around like a wild cheetah minutes earlier. Trying one more time to make friends, Susan walked over to pet her and was met with a hiss. Hurt, she pulled her hand away. Evan hadn't seemed to notice.

"Sure, I'm starving." She'd scrounged together a peanut butter sandwich and slightly expired yogurt for dinner last night.

"Sleep well?"

"Not really."

"Wasn't Wes's bed comfortable?"

"It was fine. I've been having nightmares over losing Dad ever since his heart attack."

"I have to be at the hospital in thirty minutes. Want to come and visit him?"

"Yes. I'll grab a quick shower as soon as I'm done. By the way, that cat of yours hates me."

"She likes everybody. It's your imagination. Have you heard from Grandma Audrey?"

"She's doing fine. She's volunteering at a shelter for abused women down there in Florida. She still pops into Hemingway High a few times a week to help out the new dean."

"What a trooper. I'm glad she's gotten a second wind."

"She's lucky she isn't sitting in a jail cell for the next twenty years. I'm going to take a shower."

After the shower, she ran the blow dryer through her chin-length blond waves. She was considering growing her hair. After all, if Evan and Cara did get married, she'd love to splurge on an updo. *At the rate he's moving, I'll rival Rapunzel by then.* Under the bright vanity lights, she was dismayed to notice her roots peeking out. Her extended stay in St. Louis had caused her to miss her regular hair appointment. She pulled on her stretchy jeans and a pink velour pullover.

"Mom, you ready?"

"Coming. Just got to grab my purse."

Evan flipped off the lights and ushered her out the door. "We can walk. If we cut through the parking garage, it's five minutes door to door."

They crossed a shaded street and walked half a block, passing a few morning joggers.

"Will you be home for dinner or are you staying to eat with Dad?"

Evan walked fast and she tried to hide the fact that she was out of breath when she responded to his question. "I'll play it by ear. If Dad's not too tired, I'll stay." *Besides, there's nothing in your refrigerator but eggs and protein powder. I'll take my chances with hospital food.*

When they got to the parking garage, Evan led her through a back stairway to the third floor. "If I have a chance, I'll come by." He gave her a kiss on the cheek, then continued up the stairs.

The corridor was bustling with the change of shift. Nurses were coming and going, and she passed a phlebotomist entering a patient room. Susan heard a familiar female voice as she approached Mike's room.

"Lacey? What are you doing here?"

"I was checking on a situation and remembered you said your husband was up here, so I took a minute to pop in and see if he needed anything."

"That was thoughtful. I know how busy you must be."

"The book publicity work has been a bit overwhelming, but in the end, my job as a dietician is my bread and butter. Besides, I love what I do."

Mike was propped up in his bed, more pamphlets on his tray table. He was holding a gridded paper. "Miss Daniels was showing me how to keep a food diary."

"I was telling Mike he needs to add more fruits and vegetables to his diet, and limit red meat. I was also telling him about meat alternatives, like what you heard in my food demos and lectures."

Mike's hair was damp and he smelled hospital clean. Susan assumed a nurse had been by to give him a sponge bath and hoped he wasn't expecting that kind of attention from her once he got home.

Mike said, "I haven't had much appetite at all the past few days. Not even a bacon cheeseburger sounds tempting at the moment."

Lacey said, "You'll get your appetite back as you continue to heal. Let me know if I can do anything for you." She handed him a business card and slipped out.

"Mike, you're looking better," said Susan. His face was thinner and paler than normal, stubble dotting his face like moss on the dark side of a tree, but the clean hair and fresh hospital gown were a step in the right direction. She noticed a bright bunch of flowers in a vase on the nightstand. Who are these from? They're so cheerful."

"Cara stopped by last night when she finished her shift."

"She's so thoughtful. Evan thinks you'll be home soon."

"Home? That'll be a while. I hate being a burden on Evan."

"He doesn't look at it like that. Wes is staying with his girlfriend while we're in town so we have his room to use. Evan is so busy he comes home only to eat and sleep. We won't be in the way."

"I'm using up all my vacation and personal time. What if I need more time to recover? We can't manage for long without my salary. I'm not old enough to collect social security and full pension."

"Don't worry about it now. I could always substitute. I kept my teaching license current and, God knows, I have connections at all the schools in town. I'll give Antonio Petrocelli a call when we get home. He owes me one and he's always needing substitutes at his school." She wondered if Mike would be okay at home if she were to leave him alone all day. Would he need a nurse to help him? She hoped their insurance covered that if necessary. Mike had already cut back his hours after his last heart attack and they'd basically been living paycheck to paycheck.

"How was the memorial service?"

"The synagogue was packed. He had a lot of friends and colleagues. We went back to the house afterwards for a little while."

"Have they figured out how he died?"

"Not yet. They ruled out the son. Judith Potter thinks Dr. Schmidt was having an affair. I saw a woman sobbing in the back of the synagogue, then watched her drive away in a blue Grand Marquis before the service ended. She was bundled head to toe in a black tweed coat and scarf. Why didn't she come inside, or go back to the house? Did *she* kill him?"

"If she killed him, why would she be crying? She'd have left Dodge by now if she were smart. What about the wife? It's always the wife, you know."

She was about to give him a swat before she caught sight of the IV in his arm. "Very funny. Gail seems genuinely distraught."

"I'm just saying things aren't always how they seem. You of all people know this. I'm glad you're not wrapped up in this murder investigation, if that's what it's turning out to be."

"Brian thinks his father was seeing a woman out in Clayton. When I dropped off food for Gail, there was a blue car in the driveway, like the one I saw leave the synagogue. It has to be the same person."

"Good morning, Mr. Wiles." A young, bright-eyed nurse stood at the doorway. "Time to check your vitals. How are we feeling this morning?"

"I don't know how you're feeling, but I've been better. This incision on my leg is killing me, and my chest itches."

"They had to use a vein from somewhere. I'll change the bandage for you." The nurse set to work.

"Susan, I'm going to take a nap. You should go back to Evan's."

Reluctant to leave, but wanting Mike to rest, she kissed him on the cheek and squeezed his hand. "I'll come back later."

She walked down the corridor toward the elevator. In a corner, mysteriously huddled together, she saw Judith, Lacey, and Boston talking. She ducked behind a food cart, convinced she was hidden from their view. She strained to hear.

Judith said, "Boston, the address I gave you, did you follow up?"

"No. I chickened out and destroyed it."

"You're never going to know if you don't follow up on this lead. Do you want to find her or not?"

"Neil Schmidt stole from you. We'll expose him, dead or alive." Judith checked and ignored the beep on her phone.

Lacey said, "I think he got what was coming to him, don't you? Did you find anything on the laptop?"

"I'm sifting through it now along with the files. Boston's helping me. I've got all the original consent forms."

Judith pulled a notepad and pen from her pocket. "Here's the address again. Go see if we're right, Boston."

"Okay. I have one more patient to check on and I'll go."

Susan accidently bumped into the cart, making a rattle that reverberated throughout the corridor.

"What's that?" said Judith.

"It came from over there." Lacey pointed toward the cart. Susan held her breath. Judith started toward the cart. Susan trembled, trying not to bump the cart yet again. She could push the cart at Judith and make a run for it, dash into the open patient room behind her, or…

Ding. "Judith, come on. The elevator's here," said Lacey.

Susan let out her breath and watched the threesome disappear behind the elevator door. She unkinked herself and stood up just in time to avoid the cafeteria worker who was delivering the dinner trays.

*Boston, Lacey, and Judith are all in on something. Neil Schmidt was doing something shady...they have his laptop and files...Lacey consulted with the psychology department...*It was time to follow Boston and see where that address, the same one he crumbled and threw into the fireplace at Gail's, would lead.

Chapter 9

Susan knew Boston parked at the apartment and walked to the hospital just as Evan did. She hustled back through the parking garage to Evan's apartment building, calling an Uber on the way. Proud of her new found ability to summon a ride with her app, she met it just outside the parking lot gate.

"Ma'am, you want me to sit here with the motor running? You know you'll pay whether we move or not?"

She'd pictured Uber drivers as young and hip millennials, but this guy was at least Mike's age, wearing a nylon jacket and a *Make America Great Again* baseball cap. Perhaps Uber driving could work as a side job for Mike if he had to quit the city permits office. Did they even have Uber back in Westbrook? She'd never heard of it until Evan downloaded the app on her phone a few days ago.

"Keep the motor running. Now, you see that gray Toyota over there? On the other side of this gate? As soon as the driver gets in, be ready to follow him, discreetly of course."

"Like some sort of spy or something?"

"Exactly."

The driver put on the sunglasses which had been hanging on the visor. "Is there danger involved? What if this guy has a gun or something?"

"Trust me. He's a doctor. He took an oath not to kill anyone."

Boston emerged from the street and got into his car. Susan slunk down in the back seat in case Boston happened to look in, which with the tinted windows, would have proven difficult. They pulled out and followed the gray Toyota. As they approached the first traffic light, Susan said, "It's yellow. Speed up so we don't lose him." The Uber driver gunned the engine, just making it before the light turned. *I think he's enjoying this.* They headed away from the medical complex. The buildings became more run down the further north they drove.

"Is this area dangerous?"

"Not if you're inside a locked car. I wouldn't go walking alone at night in this place if I were you."

"He's turning, stay close."

The driver let out a sigh, then skillfully followed the Toyota past Church's Chicken, McDonald's, and a run-down playground. He turned into a strip mall and parked in front of a hair salon. Boston went inside.

"Do you want me to wait for you?"

"Yes, please." Susan waited a few minutes, then squirmed out of the back seat and worked her way to the front of the salon. Through the front window, she saw Boston talking to a middle-aged black woman who was busy cutting a client's hair. The woman was tall and thin, skin the color of milk chocolate, with cropped hair dyed red in the front. She wished she could hear the conversation. Boston stood beside the woman while she finished, then followed her behind a closed door.

Susan was about to go back to the Uber, when she heard a door creak from behind the building. Carefully, she worked her way around the corner where she saw Boston speaking to the hair dresser. She stared at Boston, frozen for a moment. Then the hairdresser threw her arms around Boston and they embraced for what seemed like ages. The woman looked too old to be a girlfriend, but too young to be his mother. Who else would he be hugging?

Susan jumped when she heard a car horn spit out a series of short beeps. She realized it was the Uber and worked her way back to the car.

"Lady, your tab is climbing and I can't stay here all day."

"I'm coming." She crammed herself back into the Uber, wondering about what she had just seen and how it may or may not be related to Neil Schmidt's murder.

The driver dropped her off at the hospital. She took the elevator to the third floor and looked in on Mike. *Fast asleep. The more rest, the quicker his recovery.* Her stomach was growling and she felt shaky. The nurse who'd been in earlier came back to check on Mike.

"Is he going to be okay? He looks so pale."

"He's right on track. In a few days you'll notice a big change. Meanwhile, how are you feeling? Are you taking care of yourself?"

"I've got a bit of a headache. Blood sugar issues."

"You have to take care of yourself or you won't be able to help your hubby. Go eat something. I'll call you if there's anything to be concerned about."

If she hurried, she could grab a bite and catch Lacey's lunch time talk down in the cafeteria. Feeling lonely, she was pleased to see Valerie in the cafeteria line.

"How's Mike?"

"He's resting. The nurse said I should eat something. She'll call me if there's any change."

"I put my stuff down at the table in the corner. Lacey's going to demonstrate how to pack a healthy lunch for work."

After purchasing her grilled cheese sandwich and tomato soup, she followed Valerie to the table. Lacey, wearing a green apron, her blond hair held in place with a headband, had already begun her demo.

Valerie said, "She's got whole wheat tortillas and is stuffing them with sprouts and avocado."

Susan looked at the greasy sandwich in front of her and tried to shield it with her hand as she ate.

Lacey said, "If it's not avocado season, you can substitute hummus, which can be purchased premade. Whole Foods sells it, but it's much less expensive at Schnuck's."

Susan whispered, "If Mike goes back to work, I'll have to start packing him healthy lunches."

"What do you mean by *if?*"

"He's worried he may not be up to going back."

"Nonsense. He's not a firefighter, is he? Concertmaster of the Philharmonic? Member of the SWAT team?"

"No, he works in the city permits office."

"I rest my case."

When Lacey finished her demo, she came over to their table. "I see I have some devoted students. I hope you're trying my recipes. Mr. Wiles will need some convincing based on my visit with him this morning."

Valerie said, "I made that black bean and rice recipe for Jazzy and Elijah and they loved it. Jazzy took the leftovers for lunch yesterday."

Susan said, "I'm taking notes for when we get home. Mike doesn't know what he has in store." She ate the last bite of her sandwich.

"I've got to run up to the psychology department. Hope to see you at my next talk."

"What do you do for the psychology department again?" asked Susan.

"I consult. Investigating the role of nutrition in mental health, stuff like that."

"You worked with Dr. Schmidt, right?"

"Yeah. Now I'm working with Dr. Potter. She has some interesting research going on."

"Regarding what?" asked Valerie.

"She's looking at twins separated at birth who were fed different types of diets growing up and how it affected their personality traits."

"How did she come up with that? I mean, isn't it hard to find twins who have been separated that way?"

"The hospital has birth cards which she sorted through years ago looking for what she needed. Now, of course, you can find the info on line. She contacted adoption agencies for matches and got consent from the families involved. It was all done on the up and up. Dr. Potter is ethical, unlike some researchers who will do anything to get published. Of course, she had to expand her search to other hospitals around the state to get a large enough sample size."

Lacey packed her things into her satchel. "My hummus wrap is going to go to waste. Would one of you like to take it home?"

"Sure," said Valerie. "I'll surprise Jazzy and pop over to the station with lunch. Two days in a row. Her coworkers will be jealous."

"Great. Gotta go." Lacey disappeared through the cafeteria door.

"That one's a ball of energy. Susan, want to come with me? It's not far from here."

She checked her phone. No messages from the nurse. "Yeah. I could use the company."

When they got to the police station, they were told Detective Lowe was interviewing a witness and would be finished shortly. Valerie and Susan took a seat in the plastic chairs outside her office door.

"Do you think it's a witness in Neil Schmidt's murder case?"

"Jazzy's usually juggling several cases at once. Maybe."

The door opened. Valerie's daughter said to the witness, "You're over on Clayton Lane Court if I need to swing by, correct?"

"Yes. Anything I can do to help."

"It's the first lead we've gotten in this case. Five foot ten or so, slim build…"

"I wish I could have seen more, but he was wearing that thick puffer jacket with the hood pulled up. He had to be up to no good, snooping outside Neil's office like that."

"I'm glad you decided to come forward to help solve your friend's murder."

When the witness stepped out of the door, Susan knew immediately it was the person she'd seen at the synagogue. The one driving the blue Grand Marquis. She recognized his tweed coat, and now realized it was a man she'd seen, not the object of Neil Schmidt's extramarital affair.

She turned to Valerie. "I'll bet he was suspicious of his wife's affair and was spying on Neil to verify it. He happened to spot Neil Schmidt's murderer? How fortuitous."

"Or, he's the killer and this witness story is meant to keep the police off the track."

"Neil's son Brian said he overheard his father breaking up with someone over the phone. If his lover was angry, she may have spilled the beans to her husband, making him angry enough to kill. Or, perhaps the wife herself was the killer and this man was trying to stop her." *I have to get some solid sleep. My mind is running on fumes.*

Detective Lowe stood in the doorway. "Mom, what are you doing here?"

Valerie said, "Hey, Jazzy, we brought you lunch. It's a healthy hummus wrap made by the famous Lacey Daniels."

"Lacey Daniels?"

"The author of the book I've been talking about. *The Lazy Vegetarian.* She's also a dietician and Susan and I have been going to her lectures and food demos."

"Oh, yeah. The rice and beans lady. You packed me lunch yesterday. Thanks. I was going to make due with a candy bar and a Coke."

Susan said, "Did you find a witness in Neil Schmidt's murder case?"

"You know I can't be talking about an ongoing investigation. Your daughter's a detective."

"You sound just like Lynette."

"We seem to have a lot in common." She looked back and forth from Susan to Valerie. "I have to get back to work. Thanks for the sandwich."

Valerie said, "I'll drop off Elijah after dinner."

"Make sure he does his homework. If he says he doesn't have any, check his agenda book."

Outside the station, Susan said, "Want to go for a ride? That's the man I saw crying at the synagogue and snooping outside the Schmidt's house. I memorized the address."

"I've got a few hours to kill. Let's go."

Valerie knew the city and found the Clayton address in a hurry. Like Brian said, it was a cute brick place on a shady street. The house on one side was for sale. On the other side, an oversized tricycle was in the driveway next to a black Lincoln. The Grand Marquis was parked in the driveway. *The oversized tricycle is an idea. Maybe Mike and I can snag a couple of those when we get back to New York and get our exercise that way.*

"What are we going to say?" said Valerie. "Do we want to talk to him, or the wife?"

"Whoever answers the door. Both will give us valuable information, I'm sure."

"We can't say we know about him from the police station. Jazzy will get in trouble big time."

"Of course not. Come on. I have an idea." She rang the doorbell.

A middle-aged man, the one from the station, opened the door. He was still wearing his coat. "Can I help you?"

"I hope so," said Susan. "I'm Susan Wiles and this is my friend Valerie."

"John Rivers." His handshake was firm...businesslike.

Susan continued, "We were looking at the place next door—the one that's for sale. We saw it with the realtor yesterday and fell in love with it. Anyhow, we want to know more about the neighborhood before putting in a bid. We're knocking on doors looking for the inside scoop on the neighborhood."

"I don't know how much help I can be."

Susan stepped into the foyer. "Anything you can tell us. How are the neighbors? Do you have recycling here? Is it family friendly? We both have grandchildren who will be visiting."

"Well, it's very quiet. Same people have been in these houses for at least as long as I've been here, since 1988. It's rare houses go up for sale. The poor widow next door succumbed to cancer and her children live across the country. That's the only reason it's available."

"What does your wife think about the shopping? Are the prices at that mall we passed reasonable?"

"I don't have a wife."

"I'm so sorry. I didn't mean to bring up ..."

"No, it's not like that. I've never been married."

"Handsome man like you single all these years?" Valerie turned around slowly. "This place certainly looks as though it's had a woman's touch. Very homey."

"Thanks, but that's all me. Now, anything else I can help you with? The widow next door had a lawn guy and a handyman. Kept on top of the maintenance even after she got sick. Piece of advice, it'll go fast so if the two of you are interested in owning it you'd better move quickly."

Susan noticed the newspaper open on the table. "Do you get much crime around here?"

"No, never."

"You know; I've been following that case of the doctor who was murdered. He taught at my son's med school. I hope the students aren't at risk." She noted a wistful look cross his face.

"Um, yeah. I hope they solve it soon. Bad publicity for the hospital and the med school. They don't need that. Again."

"What do you mean, again? Do you have a connection there?"

"I'm a pharmaceutical rep. I work with many of the doctors."

"Did you know Dr. Schmidt?"

"Well, um, yes. I knew him. Wonderful man. We did business for years."

"His poor wife. And his son. We were at their house the night he died."

"You were at the Match Day reception? It's a yearly tradition. His wife insisted they keep it going, through thick and thin."

"Thick and thin?"

"All relationships have their ups and downs, right? If you wind up buying the house, you'll both have to drop by for a drink."

"Thanks, we hope that'll be the case. We appreciate your time."

Susan followed Valerie out to the car. "What do you think? No wife?"

"That place was mighty cozy looking. Did you notice the artwork? I think he's gay." Valerie started the car.

"What? Isn't that stereotyping?"

"He had one of those rainbow stickers on his briefcase by the coat rack. Good for him."

"If that's true, it kind of blows our theory out of the water doesn't it?" Susan felt the disappointment in the pit of her stomach.

"Not necessarily. I heard a story on Dr. Phil about a guy having an affair with a man while he was married. The wife attempted to murder him."

"If Gail Schmidt knew, she'd have been very embarrassed for sure. It's bad enough your husband is seeing another woman, but a man? After being married all those years?"

"You're thinking she's a suspect?" said Valerie.

"She had motive and opportunity."

"We don't know whether or not she was aware of an affair. Remember? Brian was trying to shield her. Besides, a man was snooping outside Neil's office."

"This guy is a pharmaceutical rep. He'd have access to drug samples, right?"

"So it's either Gail, the wife, or John, the ex-lover." Valerie stated it as though it were non-negotiable.

"Or Brian, the angry son. Or Judith Potter," added Susan. "Revenge or jealousy?"

Valerie looked at the dashboard clock. "I've got to get to Elijah's school. I don't like him waiting out front while all the other kids are picked up first. I'll drop you off. Do you want to go back to your son's apartment, or to the hospital?"

"The hospital. I want to see how Mike is doing. He should be getting released soon."

Chapter 10

The next morning, Mike was scheduled to be released. Susan woke up extra early and ate breakfast with Evan. She'd tidied up the room and was excited to have Mike with her again.

"Evan, have you heard any more about Dr. Schmidt's murder?"

"The police were at the hospital yesterday. Something about a break-in in Dr. Schmidt's office."

"What do you think they were after? Do you think it was the murderer who broke in?"

"I'd assume nothing."

"Perhaps someone was after his research."

"Last I heard, it's been years since he had anything published. I doubt it."

"What about his wife? Did she have a key?"

"How would I know?"

She continued to grill Evan. "Do you think she suspected her husband was having an affair?"

"Where are you getting this from? You've got too much time on your hands, Mom. Let's go."

She pulled her scarf tight as soon as they exited the building. The wind was whipping and the cold air stung her cheeks. Good thing Evan didn't have far to walk during the snowier months. "Cara brought Dad flowers the other day. We both like her a lot, you know."

Evan picked up the pace. When they arrived at the hospital, Mike was propped up, a full breakfast tray in front of him.

"Dad, how are you feeling?"

"I've been better, but I'm ready to get out of here."

Susan took a forkful of the eggs. Cold and rubbery. No wonder he didn't eat.

Evan said. "Anything you need?"

"A new ticker maybe."

"You've got the equivalent of a refurbished engine in your chest now. Comes with a thirty-year warranty as long as you maintain it. I have to get to rounds. I'll come by when you're ready to go."

"Mike, you have to eat something. What about the toast?"

"Seriously? Hard as a rock and cold when it got here."

"I can run downstairs and get you a bran muffin."

"No thanks."

"I heard there was a break-in. Neil Schmidt's office. I wonder what they wanted."

"Who knows. Anyhow, can you help me get dressed?"

"Shouldn't we wait for the doctor?"

"I'm anxious, what can I say."

She was in the process of gathering his clothes, when the doctor walked in with Wes and a few others. *This must be rounds, like Evan has to do.* She excused herself and took a walk down the hall to the psychology department. Dr. Schmidt's office was sealed with yellow tape across the door. She was surprised to see Brian outside.

"Brian? How are you holding up?"

"Okay. I found the phone we were looking for in Dad's office back home. I was able to figure out the password, my birthday, how original, and I got into his texts. Sick. The last text was sent Match Day morning. She wanted him to fly out and meet her at a sales convention in San Francisco."

"She could have been anywhere when she sent that text."

"I checked. I googled the hotel. There *was* a medical sales convention that weekend."

"That means?"

"His lover had an alibi. She didn't kill him."

She didn't mention her suspicions regarding the gender of his father's lover.

"Brian, do you think it's possible your mom found out and…"

"Killed my Dad? No way. Mom's an open book. I'd have noticed if she'd suspected anything like that."

"Of course, you would have. I didn't mean to imply anything. Do the police have any leads?"

"That black detective came by the house yesterday. I heard her tell Mom that they were pretty sure he'd died of a digitalis overdose."

"That's a heart drug, right?"

"Yeah, I guess."

"Your Mom could have gotten some from your father's bag, right? With the affair and all…"

"Excuse me?" Gail Schmidt stormed around the corner. "I come by at the request of the police and this is what I get? What are you doing implying I killed my husband! How dare you. And I didn't have access to digitalis or any other drug. My husband didn't have drugs lying around like that."

"But…" Susan felt her face heat up.

"And I knew about the affair. I've known for many years. "Did you ask yourself why now? If I wanted to kill him over the affair, I'd have done it a decade ago."

"Did you know he was seeing a man?" Susan didn't mean to blurt it out like that. She watched the color drain not from Gail's face, but from Brian's.

Brian said, "A man? That's disgusting. You're lying."

A nurse passed by, turning her head like a rubbernecker at a traffic accident. Gail took a deep breath and lowered her voice. "It's true. Your Dad had needs that I couldn't meet. John filled that role. It didn't mean our marriage wasn't real or that we didn't love each other."

Susan was floored. Gail Schmidt *knew* her husband had been seeing a man for a decade and simply accepted it.

Brian said, "I'm getting out of here. That's so gross. You knew and never told me."

"What was the point? Your Dad loved you with all his heart. We were his family."

Brian stormed down the corridor and pounded the elevator button.

"You had to stick your nose where it didn't belong? If someone intentionally killed Neil, it certainly wasn't me or Brian. We are a family. Were a family." She stormed down the corridor. Brian had already disappeared behind the elevator doors.

The last thing she'd wanted was to cause the Schmidt family more pain and now she'd created a chasm the size of the Grand Canyon between Gail and her son. She was only trying to help. Gail, Brian, and John were off the suspect list. Wasn't that worth something?

Wait. Just because there was a medical convention in San Francisco and John claimed to be there doesn't mean he *was* there. She should double check about John and the conference.

She saw Wes coming down the corridor.

"Mr. Wiles is ready to go. The attending just signed the discharge papers."

"Thanks, Wes." She went to Mike's room and gathered his things. She stuffed the health brochures and discharge papers into her purse.

Evan had gone home to get his car, which was waiting out front when the wheelchair rolled through the sliding glass doors. Susan held Cara's flowers like they were fine china, slipping into the back seat with the grace of a drunk elephant.

"Dad, if you feel dizzy or have any pain, have Mom text your doctor or me right away."

"Pain? Remember those dolls Lynette used to have on her bed? I feel like Raggedy Andy sewn together with too tight stitches and a set of encyclopedias sitting on my chest. Not to mention I've had a sore throat since the operation."

"You'll be looking like a rosy-cheeked Cabbage Patch Kid in no time," said Susan. She was feeling a bit light headed herself.

Evan helped get Mike settled, then left Susan with instructions. "Get him to drink fluids and eat what he can manage. He needs lots of rest, but he doesn't have to be bedridden. He'll get a blood clot if he lays in bed all day. Text if you need anything. I'll be back for dinner."

Mike sat in front of the TV with his feet propped up and soon nodded off. She ducked into a quiet corner and googled medical conventions in San Francisco. Sure enough, she found the itinerary. John Rivers was a moderator, for more than one session. Three suspects off the list. Verified.

Chapter 11

"Mike, you've been out of the hospital nearly a week now and you have yet to get out of this bed. Why don't you take a shower and shave? That'll make you feel better." She pulled his razor from his travel bag. "And you smell like a sweaty old man."

"What's the point. I'm not going anywhere."

"The point is, if you don't get up and start walking and doing the things the doctor told you, you're never going to get better. You want to get home to Westbrook, right?"

"I don't feel good. Let me go back to sleep."

"At least come into the dining area. I'll make you some…"

"Egg whites and dry whole wheat toast? No thanks."

Susan closed the door behind her. Evan had already gone to the hospital and she was left alone with a lethargic husband and hostile cat. She'd tried out some of the recipes from Lacey's book and they were delicious, but Mike wouldn't bite. His face was looking thin and she was sure part of his lethargy was due to his lack of interest in eating. Or was it the other way around?

She poured herself a bowl of Cheerios and coffee. The Cheerios reminded her of Mia, who she missed desperately. She was getting stir crazy and longed to sleep in her own bed. She'd tossed and turned all night worrying that Mike wouldn't regain enough strength to work again. The financial implications were overwhelming. Thank God their house was paid off, but there were taxes and maintenance, in addition to medical expenses. When she brought her food to the table, Mittens jumped off the cat tree and ran behind the couch, making her crave the affection of Johann and Ludwig once again. She really missed her cats. And her granddaughters.

Her phone rang. "Valerie, hi. He's okay, but he has yet to get out of bed. I know, it's the worst thing for him, lying around like this. I don't know how to motivate him, and Evan's at work so much, I'm going crazy stuck in this apartment. I don't know. I guess it's okay to leave him for a few hours. It's not like he needs me here while he sleeps. I'll meet you there."

She rinsed out her bowl and jumped into the shower. She felt like a kid going on a field trip, ramped up over going to the mall with Valerie. She could use a few new clothes, being she'd come with a weekend's worth of outfits and was washing underwear every other day. Maybe she'd even pick up a few new t-shirts for Mike.

"Mike, I'm going to the mall with my friend Valerie. You'll be okay, right? Can I bring you back anything? A book? Some chocolates?"

"Nah. Just hand me the remote."

"There's cereal in the kitchen, and skim milk if you get hungry. Want me to bring you a bowl before I leave?"

"Nah. Have fun."

"Are you sure you'll be okay by yourself? I'm nervous about leaving you."

"I don't need a babysitter."

Susan gathered her purse and jacket, then waited downstairs in front of the gate.

"This is the best outlet mall in the area," said Valerie. "It's a twenty-minute ride, but worth it. It gets crowded on Saturdays so it's good we got an early start."

They drove down Interstate 64, then exited into Chesterfield, a more rural area. The trees were mostly winter-bare, but the sky was bright, brush-stroked with swirls of cirrus clouds.

"It feels so good to be out of that apartment. Mike is doing nothing to help himself and I'm tired of nagging."

"Show him you're moving on and aren't going to sit around doting on him. When he gets bored of the pity party, he'll perk up. You'll see."

"What if something happens to him while I'm gone?"

"He's got a phone, and the hospital is around the corner."

They reached the mall mid-morning. Susan felt an adrenaline rush. Ann Taylor, Skechers, Vera Bradley…all her favorites.

"I could use a new pair of shoes," said Valerie. Let's duck in here.

Susan had never seen so many Skechers in one spot before. The tiny store was dense with tall metal shelves covered in shoe boxes. Susan grabbed handfuls of them and sat on a bench to try them on.

"Those look nice! I had some of those memory foam ones and they were comfy as down pillows under my feet." Valerie rummaged through a shelf of slide-ons.

Susan walked around, looking down at the mirror and turning her foot to view various angles. "I like them. They come in blue also. Which do you like better?"

"The blue hides the dirt better. Do you like these?" She held up a pair of soft, black slip- ons.

"They look comfy."

"Not too old ladyish?"

"Nope. Lynette has a similar pair." Susan walked up and down the aisle, a blue shoe on her left foot, a pink one on her right. From the next aisle, she heard a familiar voice. She strained to hear the conversation.

"How we were kept apart for so long, I still don't understand. Even my parents were surprised when I told them what I'd found out."

"It's water under the bridge. At least now we're together. And I want to buy you some doctor shoes. What size do you wear?"

Susan recognized the voice as Boston's. Who was he talking to? The hairdresser? She pulled a shoe box off the shelf and peeked through. Cropped red hair, milk chocolate skin. Yes, it was the woman he met at the beauty salon. What was Boston doing here on a Saturday with this older woman? If he was anything like any of the men she knew, he would have to be in love to agree to getting dragged around any mall, let alone an outlet mall the size of a small town.

Valerie came down the aisle holding up a pair of miniature sneakers. "These were on the kids' aisle and they're Elijah's size. Half what Jazzy usually pays for his sneakers. I'm going to pick up a size bigger too. He's growing like a weed these days. They had some cute girl shoes, too. You should bring some home for your granddaughters."

"I'll take a look. Valerie, in the next aisle, that's Boston Talmich with the woman I saw him talking to outside the hair salon last week."

"He's the psychology resident, right? The one Lacey and Judith know?"

"That's him. I can't figure out if she's his girlfriend or what."

Valerie peeked through between the shoebox spy hole. "Could be a sister."

"There's something going on between him, Judith, and Lacey. Judith gave him the address to find this woman. How would she know about a sister or whoever while Boston didn't?"

"We could ask Lacey. Say we ran into him with this woman and wondered who she was."

"She'd think we're just a pair of snoopy old ladies. He said his parents were surprised. I wonder if they live in town."

"Are you taking those?" Valerie pointed to the blue sneaker.

Susan looked at the price. They were a bargain, no doubt, and under normal circumstances she'd never have given it a second thought. Now she considered her bank account.

"I don't know."

"They look great and they are quite a deal. If you need them, get them."

Susan scooped up the box and joined Valerie at the register, fishing out her credit card. By the time the bill came due, maybe Mike would be back at work.

"Starbuck's? My treat," said Valerie. Susan followed her around the corner and they got in line. "I wish they had those pumpkin lattes year-round."

"Those are my favorite, too."

They gathered their drinks and found a booth. Valerie had sprung for a couple of cheesecake brownies to go along with the coffee. "You don't have to tell your husband about these."

"At this point, I wish he'd eat anything. I'm worried."

"My sister got like that after her back surgery years ago. The more she laid around, the worse she felt. The doctor said she was depressed."

"Did she snap out of it?"

"Honestly? She wound up going on antidepressants. That's what pulled her out of it."

"No shame in that. If this keeps up much longer, I'll talk to Evan about it." She took a bite out of the heavenly brownie. "Hey, look. Boston and that woman are coming in here."

After getting coffee, Boston and the woman took the only available seats—the booth behind Susan and Valerie. Not that she was eavesdropping, but Susan strained to hear the conversation.

Boston said, "Guess we have some things in common. We both got our coffee with skim milk and three packets of sugar. I usually get cracks about how much sugar I'm using."

"Nothing wrong with a little sweetness. Speaking of which, I'm so glad you found me. After all this time, I never expected…"

"We're together now, and I'm going to see justice is done. Step one already accomplished."

"You mean that doctor who…"

"He paid the price. Karma has a way of catching up to you. I've got two colleagues helping me piece together the rest."

"You think he's still alive? That we'll all be together?"

"I do."

Chapter 12

When Susan got back to Evan's apartment, Mike was asleep, still in the spot where she'd left him. Relying on her credit card, she'd picked up two new t-shirts and a pullover sweater for him, which she placed on top of the dresser. Looking at him lying in bed, she longed for the old Mike. In all the years they'd been together, she'd never seen him this lifeless.

She pulled out her tablet and searched *depression after illness.* Surprisingly, it was quite common. She was struck by a statistic from the American Heart Association stating about 25% of people undergoing heart surgery experience depression as a result. *Cardiac Depression. It even has its own name. Being depressed puts him at higher risk for cardiac death?* Now she was panicked. Becoming a widow was truly her worst fear. Reading on, she realized she had been encouraging the right things, a healthy lifestyle, exercise, a routine…but perhaps she hadn't been persistent enough. Taking a deep breath, she headed back to the bedroom, determined to turn things around.

"Mike, wake up. Look what I bought at the outlet mall."

Mike grumbled. "Leave me alone. I'm tired."

"Get your bottom out of that bed. We're going for a walk." She shook him, not so gently.

"Oww. That hurt." He rubbed his shoulder. "You may be going for a walk, not me."

"At least get up and come sit with me in the living room."

"I said leave me alone!" He pulled the covers up to his chin, and rolled over.

The rarity of Mike raising his voice at her stung especially hard. She left the room, pulling the door shut behind her. She plopped onto the sofa, and fought with the three TV remotes, and cried.

"Mom, I'm home." Evan put his backpack on the table and scooped up Mittens. "Did you have fun at the outlet mall?"

She wiped her eyes before answering. "Yes. Found a new pair of shoes, see." She held up her foot. "You're home early."

"Yeah. That doesn't happen often. How's Dad doing?"

"I'm really worried about him. I'm too young to be a widow. He won't get out of bed and he barely eats anything. He won't take a walk with me. Short of hoisting him off the mattress myself, I don't know what to do. How long before he feels better?"

"He should be nearly back to his old self by now. Tired, yes, but bedbound? It's going to delay his recuperation."

"You said he was going to get a blood clot if he didn't get up."

"That's a real risk. I'll talk to him."

"I was reading about cardiac depression. Maybe he needs antidepressants."

"I don't know much about that. You could make an appointment over at the hospital. Boston does clinic hours there, I think."

"I doubt Dad will agree to seeing a psychiatrist."

"Then you go and find out what you can do to help him get out of it."

Her phone vibrated. "It's Lynette and the girls." She had recently learned how to use FaceTime and was thrilled to see Annalise waving at her. "Hi, honey. I miss you so much."

"Miss you so much." Annalise blew her a kiss. "When are you coming back?"

"Soon, honey. How's school?"

"Good."

"Is your mommy there?"

Lynette appeared on the screen. "Hi, Mom. You doing okay? How's Dad? I tried to call him, but he didn't pick up."

"He's in a funk. I think he's suffering from depression."

"Nonsense. Dad? Depressed? He's just feeling tired from the surgery. He's been through a lot."

"I thought I'd try to get him to see a psychiatrist."

"Are you kidding? He'll never go for it. Annalise made him a card. I'll send it along with some of her artwork. We'll make cookies to send, too. That'll cheer him up."

Susan felt her own heart sink. Lynette wasn't here and she couldn't see how serious this was. "Have you been in contact with Detective Lowe? I wonder if they're any closer to solving the murder."

"They've been inundated with cases lately. She's being pulled in many directions. I don't think they have any new leads, but that's not your problem. Get Dad to cheer up so you can both come home."

"How are Johann and Ludwig doing?"

"We brought them over here for the time being. Bought them a new scratching post. I think they miss you. Mia scares Ludwig. He hides under the bed when she starts chasing him. Mia wants to say hello."

Mia looked older in the few weeks since she'd seen her. Her silky, black pigtails were tied with red ribbons. "HI, sweetie. I miss you."

"Grandma!" Mia wasn't big on conversation and ran away after about five seconds. Evan said a quick hello to his sister and ended the call.

Susan sighed. "Lynette doesn't get it. I don't think Dad is just going to snap out of this."

"I'll call Boston and find out about the clinic."

Evan was much more likely to face problems head on than Lynette. "Thanks."

The next morning, Susan nudged Mike to wake up. "I thought I'd try that church down the block. Why don't you come with me?"

"No, thanks. I need my rest."

"How about we go over to the zoo later? It's supposed to warm up today. We can walk slowly and if you get tired, there's a tram."

"I just want to sleep."

"Don't you want to get better? What's wrong with you?"

Mike pulled the covers up and rolled over.

She got in the shower, sobbing as the warm water hit her face. She fixed herself scrambled eggs and toast, then brought a plate into the bedroom for Mike.

"I think you should talk to someone about how you're feeling. I'm going to arrange an appointment with Boston Talmich, the resident we met at Neil Schmidt's party."

"I don't need a shrink."

"Look, if you want to stay in that black hole, so be it, but I can't take much more of this. I've been by your side this whole time. The least you can do is talk to him. I'm going back to Westbrook before Easter, with or without you."

She stormed back into the dining area and crunched her teeth into her toast so hard she was afraid she'd popped off a cap. Evan was working all day and she didn't want to sit in the apartment waiting for him to come back. She walked to the corner for a Sunday paper, then finished her breakfast while leafing through it.

Lacey is doing a book signing at the Barnes and Noble this afternoon. I already had her sign my book, but it's something to do. I'll call Valerie and see if she's interested.

She met Valerie for lunch at Whole Foods. "Did the shoes fit Elijah?"

"Like a glove. They look so cute on him. Any progress with your hubby?"

"No. I'm at my wit's end."

"It was good that you called me. You have to nurture yourself before you fall apart. One of you has to be strong enough to keep things on course."

"You're right. I didn't want to sit around watching Mike sleep. How's your sandwich?"

"Not as good as the ones Lacey makes, but passable."

"Should be more than passable given the prices in this place." She took a swig of stevia-sweetened root beer and shuddered. "What if he dies, Valerie? I can't do this, worry about him like this. He's not even trying to get better. I feel...angry. And guilty about feeling angry."

"He just had major surgery and men are big babies. You have to stand by and try not to bite his head off. He'll get over it."

"I hope you're right."

"Today's lunch is on me. My weekends get pretty lonely when I'm not watching Elijah. We should get going."

The bookstore smelled of fresh coffee. The café area was packed with what she referred to as laptop campers. Lacey was set up at the opposite end of the store. A line had formed, which was fine since they had already gotten their books signed. On the table in front of Lacey, Susan noticed another of her books. *Living through the Dark: When a Loved One Commits Suicide.*

"Valerie, did you know she wrote another book?" She opened to the title page. "It came out a few years ago."

"Huh. Never heard of it. Couldn't have been nearly the hit she has with *The Lazy Vegetarian.*"

Susan leafed through the book. "It's dedicated to the memory of her sister, Emma. She lost Emma to suicide."

"That's awful. Guess now that she's got this book in the spotlight, she's thinking she can sell the other as well."

When Lacey had finished signing, Susan and Valerie approached.

Lacey smiled. "I think I've got my first groupies."

"We were in the neighborhood," said Susan. "I didn't realize you had written other books. This one looks interesting. I'm sorry for your loss."

"Yes, my sister Emma's death was a blow I have yet to recover from. We were very close, and I blame myself for not getting her the right help. I hooked her up with the wrong therapist. I'll never forgive Neil Schmidt, even after his death."

"He didn't help her?"

"Not at all. I think he drove her to her decision to take her own life."

"You blame him, then?"

"He was a quack. As bad a therapist as he was a researcher. I didn't shed any tears over his death. The man cut corners, so unethical it makes my blood boil."

"Unethical? How?"

"Never mind. I don't want to get into it. I'm heading home."

After she left, Susan asked Valerie, "Do you think that was motive for killing Neil Schmidt? I didn't realize there was a connection."

"Why wait what, three or four years? If she wanted to kill him, don't you think she'd have done it back then?"

"I wonder if there's a recent trigger. We have to find out what Neil Schmidt was working on when he died." Susan looked out the bookstore window. "Hey, isn't that Judith Potter driving the car Lacey just got into?"

"We've seen them together. It's no surprise."

"Guess you're right." She headed to the self-help section. *Surviving the Loss of a Spouse, Healing After Heartache*...Her phone vibrated.

"Mike? What? Did you call 911? I'll meet you at the hospital."

"What's wrong?"

"Mike thinks he's having another heart attack. I've got to get to the hospital. It's all my fault for leaving him alone."

"Come on, I'll drive you."

"I have to call Evan." He wasn't picking up, so she left a text.

When they got to the emergency department, they ushered Susan through the doors. Wes was with Mike.

"His EKG is normal, but we'll run some more tests. Has he been short of breath? Nauseous?"

"Really tired. He won't get out of bed."

"We'll take care of him."

Evan came through the door as they were wheeling Mike out for tests. "What happened?"

"I shouldn't have left him alone. He thinks he's having another heart attack."

"Mom, they fixed the weak part of his heart so it's unlikely. Don't panic."

"Like I said, the EKG was normal," said Wes. "Go get a cup of coffee and we'll call when the tests are concluded. Are you comfy in my room?"

"Very. I can't thank you enough, but I feel bad that it's been this long. I thought we'd be heading back to New York by now."

"Don't worry about it. I may come by and pick up some more clothes, though."

He's the student who scored so low on his Step exam he has to go to North Dakota for residency. When he left, she voiced her concerns to Evan. "Why is Mike being treated by a med student? Where's the doctor?"

"He's under the care of an attending, who I'm sure will be in shortly."

"Then that's good, right? If it were serious, the real doctor would have been in there."

"The EKG was normal, and Dad is sitting up, talking. I'm not too worried."

Susan remembered Valerie was still sitting in the waiting room. "Evan, I have to tell my friend what's happening."

"Go on. He'll be here when you come back. Mom, I'll check back with you as soon as I hear anything." Evan gave her a peck on the cheek. "Try not to worry."

She went out to the waiting room.

Valerie stood up. "Susan, how is he?"

"They're running tests. The EKG was normal. Evan thinks he's going to be okay."

"Want to get some coffee?"

"Sure."

Trying not to worry was like trying not to think of elephants. Susan's chest felt like a boa constrictor was squeezing her heart.

"He'll be okay. It's probably just them healing pains like when I had my gallbladder surgery. Feels worse before it gets better."

"I'm going up to the psychiatric wing to see if I can get him an appointment at the clinic ASAP. Then we can get coffee."

"I'm coming."

They took the elevator up. When the doors opened, Susan immediately spotted Boston Talmich.

"Hi, Mrs. Wiles. I though your husband was discharged?"

"He's down in the ED. Thinks he's having another heartattack."

"I'm sorry to hear that."

"It's his own fault. He wasn't getting his exercise, not even getting out of bed. All he does is sleep. I think he has cardiac depression."

"It's fairly common. Facing your own mortality coupled with the physical challenges of recuperating from surgery."

"Evan was going to talk to you about treating him."

"I have clinic hours twice a week. I'd be happy to squeeze him in."

"Does it work? Therapy I mean. I was talking to Lacey Daniels and found out her sister committed suicide. She was seeing a therapist. I think it was Neil Schmidt."

"She has referred to him as a quack on more than one occasion, so I guess it's not a secret. It was before I got here. What's that phrase my mom used to say? Don't throw away the baby with the bath water. Therapy doesn't work for everyone, but it works for many. Sometimes medication helps stabilize the brain chemicals."

"I hope you can help him."

Boston's phone rang. "Gotta go. We'll talk soon."

Valerie said, "Such a nice young man. I'd like Jazzy to meet him."

"They'd make a cute couple, for sure. Unless…"

"You seriously think that woman we saw him with was a girlfriend? She's too old and he's entirely out of her league."

They went down to the cafeteria for coffee. Susan couldn't help wondering about Lacey Daniels and Neil Schmidt. She took out her phone and googled the story. Without much effort, she found an article.

"Valerie, Lacey's sister jumped off the roof of the hospital. It says Dr. Neil Schmidt talked to her for hours trying to convince her to come down, but ultimately she jumped."

"That's awful!"

"If I was Lacey, I'd surely blame Dr. Schmidt for my sister's death and I'd be mad enough to kill. If I had a sister, I mean."

"But why now? It's been a couple of years, right?"

Susan continued scrolling through articles.

"Your coffee's getting cold."

"Wait. I think I've got something. Lacey's family filed a civil suit against Neil Schmidt. They lost. It concluded a week before Neil's death."

Valerie took a sip. "Now, that makes more sense. Would she have access to that drug?"

"Well, she runs around with Judith Potter and Boston Talmich. One of them might have been able to get it for her."

"Or maybe she didn't need a drug at all. She knows all about nutrition and herbal remedies, right? Maybe she came up with a concoction herself."

"Let's call your daughter."

"Jazzy will need more than that to take us seriously. Believe me, I've been there before with her. There was a break-in at Elijah's school last year and I called it right off the bat. The custodian did it. I told her, but she ignored me. Eventually they found proof and arrested him, but it took months."

"She has an office here, right? She went home after the book signing this afternoon. Let's see if we can get into her office."

"Like break in?"

"How about I pretend I left something in there and ask a security guard to open it?"

"Security won't let you in. You know how things are nowadays. I'm surprised there aren't metal detectors at the entrance. Think we can find out what time the night cleaning crew arrives? I think we'd have more of a chance slipping in then. Meet back here tonight?"

"It's a date."

Chapter 13

Mike's tests came back normal and by dinner time, they were back at Evan's apartment. "The doctor said it was just stress, but you have to start getting some exercise." Susan felt both relieved, and angry that Mike had put them through this.

"Mom's right. You can't lay around all day and expect to feel better. Here, I made some chicken and spinach. Baked fries, too."

Mike took a few bites. "I want to go back to New York. You don't need me hanging around day in and day out, and Wes has to miss sleeping in his own bed."

"He'd tell me if he wasn't okay with it. Take short walks with Mom. The park is just across the street and there are plenty of benches if you need to rest. That's how you'll get stronger. And you have to eat."

Mike ate his chicken and took seconds on the fries. Susan was a little annoyed that Mike refused to listen to her, but when it came from Evan…She had to stop that. The goal was getting Mike better and if it took Evan saying what to do, then so be it.

Evan put his plate in the sink. "I'm going to run over to the gym." He grabbed a protein bar from the pantry.

Mike said, "I'd like to try sitting out here on the sofa for a while. I am tired, though."

Yes. Maybe he could figure out the remote controls. Evan had explained it three times and she was embarrassed to ask again. She looked at her watch. *I hope Mike falls asleep before I have to meet Valerie outside Lacey's office.*

Mike hadn't made it to the end of *Sixty Minutes* before conking out on the sofa. Susan pulled on her coat and carefully locked the door behind her. It was creepy, walking alone in the dark. At one point, she was sure she was being followed and took the mace out of her purse. She quickened her pace and took the shortcut Evan used. When she got to the hospital, Valerie was waiting.

"How's your hubby doing?"

"I think Evan got through to him, but I'm still going to get him an appointment with Boston Talmich."

"Glad he's alright. Now, what's our plan?"

Thanks to an earlier conversation with one of Mike's nurses, they knew what time the night custodians arrived. It was Sunday night and none of the offices were open.

"Susan, let's wait around the corner. We'll be out of sight of the cameras."

They wore black clothing—Valerie's idea—and waited for the cleaning crew to come down the hall. The floor was damp and smelled like disinfectant where they waited, reinforcing their assumption that the crew had already been here and they were safe.

"I'm going to wait down there. You creep closer to the door like we planned." Susan felt like a cat, sneaking up on its prey.

When a single custodian opened Lacey's office, Valerie, farther down the hall, rammed a cart into the wall, causing an echoing clang in the silent corridor. The custodian ran out to see what it was. *Good going Valerie. With those earbuds hanging in his ears, I was afraid he'd miss the crash.*

Heart pounding, Susan snuck into the office, which was propped open with the pail and mop. She hid in the coat closet, then waited for Valerie's text. *She should be here by now. What if she got caught?* She cracked open the closet door just a bit. Before she had a chance to work herself into a full blown tizzy, she heard a soft knock on the door.

"It's me."

Recognizing Valerie's, voice, she relaxed and opened the door. "You were supposed to text me."

"Couldn't get a signal. Coast is clear. Where do we start?"

"How about right here?" Susan walked over to the shiny black desk and found a planner which had been left in plain sight. She flipped to the week of Neil's murder. "Looks like Lacey met with a lawyer several times. Here's where she went to court to hear the verdict. She drew a skull and crossbones on that square."

"I'll see if there's anything in the file cabinet." It glided open when she pulled the handle. "It's unlocked. These are all red folders." Valerie rifled through the folders, creating a pile on the floor beside her. Susan wondered if this was just a waste of time.

Valerie said, "Here's one labeled *Neil Schmidt*. All sorts of notes and photos, too."

"Let me see." They squinted to read the hand written notes.

"Want me to turn on the lamp?"

Caught by surprise, Susan felt a blow to the back of her head, then felt herself hit the cold tile.

She opened one eye, then the other, trying to focus through a blurry haze of disorientation. Her arm ached where she'd been lying on it and she wondered how much time had passed. Turning her head, she saw Valerie on the floor next to her, blood matting the hair over her forehead. "Valerie, wake up. Wake up! Are you okay?"

Valerie groaned. "What happened?"

"Someone snuck up on us while we were reading the files." She propped herself up on her elbow. "Where are the files?"

"Huh? My head hurts."

"Let's get out of here." Susan felt dizzy when she tried to stand. She took a deep breath and steadied herself on the desk. "You're bleeding."

Valerie ran her hand over her head. "I sure am."

Susan pressed the scarf she was wearing to Valerie's wound. Direct pressure. She'd heard that somewhere. "Hold that in place. Let's get out of here." She stumbled to the door, turned the handle, then yanked hard. "It's locked. From the outside!"

"I'll call for help." Valerie reached for her purse and took out her phone. "Don't tell me."

"What's wrong?"

"No signal." She reached up and grabbed the desk phone. Then she slammed down the receiver. "Someone cut the phone wire!"

Susan tried her own phone. No signal either. She banged on the door. "Help. We're stuck in here."

"No one's here, remember? And I didn't tell anyone where I was going, did you?"

"Nope. We may be stuck here all night." *By now, Evan should be home. He'll wonder where I am. I hope Mike doesn't panic if he wakes up and can't find me.* "It had to be Lacey that did this. She's the one with the key, and she knew she had things in that file she didn't want us to see." Something shiny under the desk caught her eye. "This has to be Lacey's diamond stud earring. She must have lost it while conking us out."

"A soon as we get out, we're going to the police. This has to be enough to bring Lacey in for questioning. She assaulted us!" Valerie held her head. "This really hurts. I might have a concussion or something."

Susan remembered the wisdom about not letting someone with a suspected concussion go to sleep. Her mom used to say that, though she didn't know if it still held true. *Better safe than sorry.*

"Valerie, where did you grow up?"

"Right here in St. Louis. You?"

"In New York, not far from where I live now. How did you meet your husband?"

"What's this, twenty questions? We should be figuring out how to get out of here. I feel nauseous."

Susan handed her the wastebasket. "You might have a concussion. You have to stay awake. Someone will find us in the morning."

"Who? Lacey? This is her office."

She hadn't thought that far ahead. *Lacey will deny being here.* "We'll make a run for it as soon as she opens the door. Meanwhile, you have to stay awake."

"A run? Look at us." Valerie set the wastebasket down. "Well, I met my husband in high school. Went to two proms together, attended St. Louis University together...he was my best friend. I miss him every day."

This was hitting close to home, especially because of the scare Mike had gone through earlier today. "I met him at my summer job. I waited tables at a resort in the Catskills and he was visiting with his family. He wound up staying the rest of the summer, working as a life guard, and the rest is history." She remembered how buff he looked in those red, white, and blue swimming trunks. Her own eyes wanted to close. It had been a long day, and she knew Mike and Evan would realize she was missing by now. "I'm hungry."

"Maybe Lacey's got some food stashed away in here."

"Like kale chips or gourmet granola? I'll check." Susan pulled open the bottom drawer.

"I'd eat paint about now," said Valerie.

"Holy moly, she's got candy in here! She's a fraud."

"Fraud? Right now she's my hero. Any *Almond Joys*?"

"Dark chocolate covered almonds, carob bars…wait. Here's the good stuff. Want a *Kit Kat*?" She tossed one to Valerie, who tore open the wrapper.

"A bite of heaven. What else you got?"

"She has a toothbrush and floss if you need it." Susan dug through the cosmetic bag. "Lip gloss, mascara…" She was about to close the drawer when she spotted a second cosmetics bag.

"What's in there?"

Susan unzipped the floral bag, which she recognized as the most recent Clinique gift with purchase. "Photos. Doubles of kids and young adults."

Valerie scooted closer and took the stack. "These aren't the same kids."

"Of course, they are."

"No, look. See this teenaged girl? In this photo she has a tattoo on her neck. See the spider's web?"

"And?"

"The picture that looks like her, the girl doesn't have a tattoo."

"Could be one of those temporary henna things."

"Look at these two boys, then. One has a scar over his eyebrow, the other doesn't. And they look the same age. Kids grow fast those years so I don't think in one shot he is okay, and weeks later he's got a healed scar on his face."

Susan took the photos, dozens of them, pushed up her bifocals and said, "You may be right." She went through the other photos. "Hey, I think I know him. This looks like Boston Talmich, the psych resident!"

"The hunk we followed at the outlet mall. The one with the older woman, right?"

"Yep. He's younger here, but those eyes…"

"Mmm, and those dimples. It's him. Look at the one in that other photo."

Susan looked at the details. "This boy has a dimple but it's on the left side of his mouth, not the right!"

"So Boston Talmich has a twin!"

"Neil Schmidt's research had something to do with twin studies. We heard that a few times. And we also heard the words *unethical and falsified.*"

"Do you think these belonged to Neil Schmidt and Lacey was building a case against him?"

"We don't know these were his patients. Lacey also consulted for Judith Potter. I'm not sure. If she had a case against him, why not follow through instead of turning around and killing him?"

"Losing the civil suit had to be a big blow. Perhaps she just lost it."

"Neil's death took planning. She'd have had to gotten the meds, slipped it to him…"

"Like we said, she had access to drugs and herbal hocus pocus. She had motive, and she's smart."

"What else is in there?"

"That's it."

Valerie teetered on her way to standing up. "There's a pile of papers on that chair." She picked through them. "Here's an issue of *Psychology Prime* from last fall. Look. Right on the cover. *New evidence supports nurture over nature.*" She flipped to the table of contents. "It's by Dr. Neil Schmidt!"

Susan read over her shoulder. "*Long term blind studies show new evidence that environment outweighs genes in the ultimate success of human beings. When it comes to job choice, economic stability, and overall happiness, a stable, two parent home environment is key to overcoming genetic tendencies.*"

"So he got his research published and no mention of Lacey or any other consultants."

"This is hardly a peer reviewed medical journal, but he was getting this stuff out there."

"Another reason to want Schmidt dead! Lacey already thought he was a quack."

"Judith Potter had those red folders in her hand that day in the elevator. I was told those were permissions and such. Now Lacey has photos of twins stashed away."

"If Boston had a twin that he didn't know about, one Lacey and Schmidt were concealing…"

"It's not too difficult to connect the dots."

Valerie snapped photos of the photos as well as the pages of calendar entries. "At least this phone is good for something."

"Are you sleepy now?"

"Nope. Between the adrenaline and the candy, I'm ready to finish out this all-nighter."

Chapter 14

Despite the effort, both Valerie and Susan wound up asleep in Lacey's office. Susan startled when the office door opened.

"Susan? Valerie? What are you doing in my office?" Light was streaming through the blinds and Susan stared up at Lacey Daniels. "What happened here? Why's my filing cabinet open? Why are there candy wrappers all over the floor?"

"You were robbed and the thief hit us over our heads," said Valerie.

"Lacey, we came to see you last evening," said Susan. "I had this idea about flying you up to Westbrook to do a book signing when the new senior center opens later this year. We knew it was a long shot, but we thought we'd check and see if you were here. I was so excited to ask you."

"Did you see the burglar?"

"No. The door was cracked open and when we went inside, someone bashed us over our heads and locked us in. Thank God you found us. I think Valerie has a concussion."

Lacey examined the wound on Valerie's forehead. "Do you feel dizzy? How many fingers am I holding up?"

"I'm fine. You've got to call the police."

"I will, but first, you need to get checked out by a doctor. You may need stitches for that gash." She went for the desk phone. "My phone line has been cut!"

Susan had to hand it to her. Lacey was one good actress pretending it wasn't her who'd been there last night. Trying to call from the office phone was a nice touch. "I have to call Evan and Mike. They must be worried sick." She stepped out into the hall and still couldn't get a decent signal. She ran into Wes.

"What are you doing here so bright and early Mrs. Wiles?"

"It's a long story. I have to call Mike and I can't get a signal."

"Evan is downstairs. I just saw him."

"Great." She checked in on Lacey and Valerie.

"Susan, the police are on the way. Why don't you run Valerie down to the ER?"

"I'm fine. I just want to go home and get some breakfast." Valerie rubbed her head.

"Come on, Valerie. We'll be quick." Susan winked at Valerie and led her to the elevator. "I want Evan to look at your wound. Then we've got to get to the police."

Downstairs, Susan found Evan. "I'm so sorry. You must have been worried sick!"

"Mom? I figured you'd gone to bed last night. Dad was asleep on the sofa, still sleeping when I left the apartment at the crack of dawn. What's wrong?" *Was he serious? He didn't realize she was gone?*

"Nothing. Can you look at Valerie's gash? Does she need stitches?"

He pulled on latex gloves. "Just needs to be cleaned and bandaged. It isn't too deep. What happened?"

Valerie said, "Clumsy me. Hit it on the car door when I was getting out. Thank you for saving me a wait."

When they finished, Susan called Mike, who hadn't realized she was gone either. "I'm eating breakfast with my friend, Valerie, and then we're heading to the mall. You okay?"

"Yeah. Thought I might try Evan's exercise bike for a few minutes."

She was thrilled. "Great. Set it on number one, no tension. And put on some shoes so you don't hurt your feet."

"All set?"

"All set. He's riding Evan's exercise bike."

"Well, that's a positive step, right? Come on, I'll drive."

"Do you know neither Mike nor Evan even realized I was gone last night?"

"Seriously? I suppose that's a good thing. At least they weren't worried."

"And how long would it have taken for them to call for help had we stayed locked in Lacey's office?"

"I coulda been in there for days. Unless Jazzy needs me to help her with Elijah, she don't keep tabs on me."

Valerie parked in front of the station. When they went in, they were told Detective Lowe was in her office.

Valerie took the lead. "Jazzy, did you get the report about the robbery?"

"What robbery? Mom, I tried to call you. I dropped off Elijah on my way in. I wasn't sure if you were coming by and I couldn't reach you. Was your place robbed?"

"Not mine, Lacey Daniel's office over at the hospital."

Detective Lowe shuffled through the reports on her desk. "No reports of a robbery at the hospital."

"I knew it. Jazzy, have we got something for you. Last night, Susan and I were locked in Lacey Daniel's office. She bashed me over the head." She put her hand beside the bandage on her forehead.

"Are you okay? What were you doing in her office last night?"

"Susan had to ask her something about a book signing." Susan nodded. "Anyhow, we found photos of identical twins and a magazine article about a twin study written by Dr. Neil Schmidt. Boston Talmich was one of the twins."

"You found what? She let you rifle through her office?"

"Not exactly."

"Mom! That's trespassing She could bring you up on charges."

"She doesn't know we saw them."

"If you *did* find anything relevant, it's an illegal search and the evidence isn't admissible. Haven't I taught you anything!"

Valerie pulled out her phone. "See. Here's some of the photos, and a picture of the article. As far as Lacey knows, we were there to visit and the office was burglarized. Besides, she's not going to admit to hitting us over the head."

"Then she knows you were there. I don't know how many times I've had to tell you about not snooping and staying out of police business."

Susan couldn't believe it. This was exactly the conversation she'd had with Lynette over and over again.

"But it proves she had motive to kill Dr. Schmidt. She doesn't have an alibi, does she? She had access to drugs and her office is right next to his."

"It's a far cry from proof."

"And why didn't she report the robbery?"

"Go home and don't admit to anyone what you did. And you'd better stay away from Lacey Daniels."

"Is that an order? *You* can pick up Elijah after school. My friend and I have plans." Valerie folded her arms and turned around.

"Mom!"

An officer came into the office. "Detective, we need you."

"We'll finish this conversation later."

Once they were back in the car, Valerie said, "Now what?"

Susan said, "I have to go check on Mike and see about getting him in to talk to a therapist. We're going to have to get more on Lacey all by ourselves to convince your daughter she's guilty."

Valerie dropped her off in front of Evan's building. When she went upstairs, she was surprised to hear voices. Wes was talking to Mike.

"Mrs. Wiles. I just came by to pick up more of my things. I see your husband has been exercising." The stationary bike had been pulled into the middle of the living room.

Mike was wearing scrub pants and a water bottle sat on the coffee table.

"I'm hoping he'll make a quick recovery so we can go back home and give you back your room!"

"Not a problem. I'm thinking about marrying Bethany and this is a good trial run."

"Really? Well, congratulations. I wish Evan would think that way. Cara is a real gem."

"They're a good couple. You know Evan. He doesn't make decisions lightly."

"Does your mom have grandkids yet?"

"What? No. It's just me now and that's quite a few years down the road, even if I do get married."

"No brothers or sisters?"

"Um, no. Not anymore."

Mike glared at her.

"I'm so sorry. I knew that."

"I don't like to talk about it. Let me get out of your hair." Wes went into his room.

Mike said, "You knew about the fire. Cara's mother told us at the reception."

"I'm so forgetful these days."

"Nosy, you mean."

After Wes left, Susan called Boston's clinic. He'd left a message saying he was able to squeeze Mike in. "Come on, get dressed. We're heading to the hospital."

Chapter 15

"This is the first time I walked into this place through the front door," said Mike.

"Come on, the elevator is over here. It was nice of Boston to squeeze you in."

"This isn't necessary, you know. I'm only going along with it to get you off my back."

Susan tightened Mike's belt once inside the elevator. His jeans, a just fit back in Westbrook, kept slipping down. A month ago if she'd reached into his pants like that she'd have been met with some sort of wisecrack, but now Mike just stared at the elevator panel. To her horror, when the doors opened, she was bent down, fastening the buckle. She felt heat rush to her face.

"Come on, you can walk faster than that, even in *your condition.*" She wanted to escape the humiliation as fast as possible.

"Don't rush me."

Mike's affected shuffle was trying her patience. She could swear he was deliberately taking his time. "It's right down this hall." She signed in at the clinic desk and they were shown into an office.

Boston Talmich shook their hands. "Have a seat. If you would fill out these forms, Mrs. Wiles, I can get started with your husband."

She searched for their insurance cards and checked the phone for the number of their primary care physician.

Boston said, "You can fill out the rest in the waiting room and give them to the office manager at the desk."

She was hoping she'd get to state her own concerns about Mike, but it wasn't in the cards. She noticed a framed photo on Boston's desk. "Are these your parents?"

"You're surprised. They're as white as snow and then there's me. Obviously, I'm adopted."

"I am, too! And our daughter and son-in-law adopted a little girl from China. Her name is Mia." She wanted to ask about his twin, the one whose picture she found in Lacey's files, but stopped herself.

"I couldn't manufacture better parents if I tried. Now, our session lasts 50 minutes. You're welcome to come back or to wait in the waiting room."

"Glad I brought a book with me. See you in 50 minutes."

Susan took a seat on a sofa in the waiting area. Unlike the sterile, plastic chairs that lined the waiting room in the ED, she could tell thought had gone into making this area homey. Doctors working in this field would pay attention to making the area comfortable. She was absorbed in her book when Lacey Daniels appeared.

"Mrs. Wiles. You're reading my first book."

Susan hadn't seen her come in. "Yes, very engrossing, but must have been painful to write."

"In a way it was therapeutic. I'm hoping it helps others who have suffered a loss due to suicide. I'm also trying to spread the word to check out a therapist's credentials and references before signing up for such an intimate relationship. Wish I'd done my homework."

"You can't think your sister's death was your fault?"

"I wish I hadn't hooked her up with Neil Schmidt. In retrospect, I shouldn't have trusted him. What are you doing here?"

"I brought Mike to see Boston Talmich. He's having trouble getting his mojo back since the surgery. After what you just said, I hope he's a good choice."

"Boston? He's a natural at this. I'm affiliated with an eating disorders group run by the hospital. In fact, I just finished consulting with the doctor who runs the group. I've heard raves about Boston Talmich." Her phone rang. "Excuse me. It's my publisher." She exited the waiting room.

Susan looked at her watch. Thirty minutes to go. Not seeing a restroom, she went out the door to the one she'd passed on the way in. Lacey was on her phone. Walking slowly, she overheard something.

"Now that we're in the clear, there's nothing in the way of its release. Law suit is up in smoke. Go for it."

Lacey strutted down the corridor, not noticing Susan.

What is she so happy about? Nothing in the way? Does she mean Neil being dead? Was she really talking to her publisher? If so, was she waiting to release a new book? She looked at her watch. She had about twenty minutes to kill. Lacey had several lawyer appointments on her calendar. She called Valerie.

"Hi, Val. Do you remember what law firm was listed on Lacey's calendar? Yeah, Lacey is looking guiltier by the minute. I overheard her talking to her publisher, saying the law suit was dropped. She has another book in the wings."

"I'll bet she's about to blow the whistle on Neil Schmidt's research. He was suing her to block it and now that he's dead..."

"Further motive. Now she has her sister's suicide, Neil's article that was just released, and him blocking the release of her new book."

"Bingo."

"I've got to get back to Mike. Work on how we can find out what's in that book and why it was so important for Neil to block it."

She walked back to the clinic. Mike was exiting Boston's office. "Great timing."

"Yeah. Want to get lunch?"

Happy that he had an appetite, she said, "Sure. Anywhere you want."

"Fried chicken, chips, and fried Oreos. The food trucks are outside."

Susan felt her face drop. Another flash of living life as a widow.

"Just kidding. Didn't we pass a deli coming here? Turkey on rye. Do you approve?"

She was stuck on the fried Oreos, but said, "Let's go."

"I have to drop off this prescription, first. Boston says these will help stabilize my brain chemicals or something like that."

"That's great. You'll feel better soon."

"It takes a while to get in your system. And if the side effects are bad…"

"Give it a try. If it doesn't work, we'll go from there. Did it help talking to Boston?"

"I guess. He says it's very common to be depressed after heart surgery. Any surgery or major illness can do it."

"Told you. It's nothing to be ashamed of."

"I don't want to be a burden to you or the kids. What if it happens again? What if next time I'm not so lucky and become a vegetable?"

"Don't get ahead of yourself. Evan said the bypass went well and chances are overwhelming that you won't have another problem if you take care of yourself."

They walked down the block stopping to drop off Mike's prescription on the way.

"This will be quicker than I thought," said Susan. The beauty of chain drug stores was that Mike's medical and insurance information was already on file. They were in and out in under ten minutes.

"Where's this deli?" asked Mike.

"One more block. There it is."

The Green Deli resembled an artsy Parisian café with white iron tables shielded by yellow striped umbrellas. The weather still required a jacket, but the cloudless sky and unobstructed sun meant the outdoor tables were completely occupied. She couldn't help noticing the oversized muffins and black and white cookies under the glass counter they passed as they made their way inside to a booth near the window.

Mike opened the menu. "Not quite like the delis back home. I don't see half garlic pickles anywhere."

"But they do have Dr. Brown's Root Beer." She watched the baskets of sandwiches being served, trying to decide what she was in the mood to eat. "Mike, how can I find out what Lacey Daniel's new release is all about?"

"Are you still on that sleuthing mission?"

"She has strong motive. She blames Neil Schmidt for not talking her sister off the ledge, and he was blocking the release of her new book. Working in the same office suite, she had opportunity to slip him the heart meds."

"That sweet little dietician? Come on. Plus, she's already a successful author. And she wasn't anywhere near him the night of the reception, right?"

Sweet little dietician? Her phone rang. "It's Valerie."

Mike nodded, still studying the menu.

"Really? So you found the law firm. They specialize in copyright law and what?"

Valerie said, "Maybe they were working out a settlement or something, with the number of meetings listed. I'll let you get back to lunch."

"She's guilty. I feel it in my gut."

"You can't go accusing Lacey Daniels of anything or you'll be slapped with a libel charge at the least," said Mike, interrupting her reverie.

"I know. We need more proof."

"We? You mean the police?"

"Tried them. Not interested."

"You can't keep from searching out problems, can you? Maybe I should retire so I can keep an eye on you."

"Yeah! You'll get bored like I did. Hey, you can be the Watson to my Sherlock. I like the sound of that."

Chapter 16

The next morning, Mike joined Susan and Evan at the breakfast table. Susan felt a wash of relief seeing him begin to act normal again. Evan scrambled eggs and popped whole wheat bread into the toaster. He opened a fresh can of cat food for Mittens.

"Mom and Dad, I'm off tomorrow. How about we go out for dinner with Cara? Dad, are you up to it?"

"Sure."

"There's a new Vietnamese place that some of the nurses were talking about."

"Can I eat that?"

"Why not? They use lots of vegetables and stir fry is healthy if you don't go overboard on the oil. Cara loves Asian food."

"Wes was telling me living with Bethany is like practice for marriage. I'll bet they get engaged soon. Are any of your other friends married?"

"Don't go there, Mom. I've got to go to the hospital, but I'll be back by five. I'll make a reservation. It's supposed to warm up today. You and Dad should take a walk."

Mike took to the suggestion and pulled on his baggy jeans and a sweatshirt borrowed from Evan. "I don't need a coat, do I?"

"It's still in the 50's. The last thing you need is to catch a chill." She wrapped a scarf around his neck and helped him into his jacket. Mittens meowed at him and rubbed herself against his legs.

"That cat likes me."

Susan bent down to pet her. Mittens darted into the living room and climbed up the cat tree. *She just likes men. That has to be her issue with me.* She snapped off the lights. "Let's go."

Susan held Mike's hand and supported him down the elevator and across the busy street to the park.

"Valerie said they call St. Louis the biggest little town in the country. I can see why."

"I don't get it. It's a city like any other city. Traffic, noise, and pollution."

"But look around. Now that we're in the park, you'd never guess we're in a city. Look at the joggers along the path and the bike riders. And all those strollers."

"There are bike riders and joggers in New York City, too."

"But it's so family-oriented here. I can't get over the fact that the zoo is free. If we lived here I'd be strolling Mia around looking at the gorillas every weekend. And you'd be holding Annalise's hand beside us."

Mike stopped short. Susan heard his effort at breathing and found a bench. "Let's sit for a while."

"I can barely walk across the street. How am I supposed to go back to work?"

"You're in the process of recovering. It won't happen overnight, but you're taking a step in the right direction. Get it? A step?"

Mike didn't even crack a smile. "We should add each other's names to our bank accounts. If anything happens to me, you won't be able to access my fortune."

"If you think I'm going to let you have access to my secret savings you've got another think coming. I'll leave it to you in my will. I've got enough there to cover say a night in a hotel and a couple of nice dinners." In reality, the bulk of their money sat in a joint account established nearly forty years ago when they got married.

"Let's go back to the apartment."

"We'll rest a few more minutes, then walk over to the art museum. *Then*, we'll go back. I'm in no hurry. Come on."

They continued, hand in hand, down the path, stopping every few minutes to rest.

"Let's sit here and enjoy the fresh air." Susan noticed Mike straining to breathe again. "You're doing so well."

"I'm not a baby, don't placate me."

"I didn't mean to."

"Do you know how hard this is for me?"

"That's why we're resting. We can sit as long as you need to."

"Not this. I mean the whole enchilada. I'm supposed to be the strong one, the provider. I hate not being able to drive a car. I hate invading my son's apartment. I hate having you act like I'm one of the children."

"Our vows said in sickness and health. We're partners. There have been plenty of times over the years when you took care of me."

"It's humiliating."

"I can't say I don't get angry when you refuse to help yourself recover. As long as I know you're doing what you need to do to get back to yourself, I'm patient."

"Seriously?"

"Okay, so patience isn't normally my thing, but in this case I will be. Are you feeling any effects of the antidepressants yet?"

"I don't know. Maybe a little."

"Come on. Let's head back."

Mike loosened the scarf and opened his jacket. Susan could tell he was sweating. Was it normal exertion sweat, or another heart attack sweat? She knew she'd be asking herself those sort of questions forever. She spotted a white news van.

Mike said, "Looks like the reporter is interviewing someone. Is there breaking news here that we're unaware of?"

They walked closer. "No, that's Lacey Daniels! Her new book will be released soon, I think. I bet that's what it's about." They went closer. A small group of onlookers hovered just out of the camera's range.

The reporter said, "Is it accurate to say this new book is a tell-all exposing secrets from the psychology department over at St. Agnes?"

"I'm simply showing the need to keep research ethical." She paused. "And exposing some juicy secrets."

"You're publishing this book right on the heels of your big success, *The Lazy Vegetarian.* How do you manage to be so prolific? You work as a dietician and consultant as well, correct?"

"Yes. I lecture over at the med school and consult with patients over at the hospital regarding their dietary needs. Fitting it all in can be a challenge, however, *Double Jeopardy* has been ready for release for quite some time."

"Why the delay?"

"An ongoing lawsuit by one of the researchers I exposed in my book."

"And it's now resolved?"

"It is resolved."

"We look forward to your new release, *Double Jeopardy,* hitting the bookstores tomorrow. Will you be making any special appearances?"

"I'm flying to New York in a few days to do a segment on *The Today Show*. Tomorrow, I'll be signing books at Barnes and Noble right around the corner, at noon."

"Best of luck, Miss Daniels. We'll be watching for your name on the bestseller list."

The lights turned off. "It's a wrap," said the reporter. He thanked Lacey, then got back into the van. Susan and Mike made their way to her.

"Where's my other groupie?" said Lacey.

"Just me and Mike. We were walking in the park and happened upon the interview."

"Mr. Wiles, I'm glad to see you getting your exercise. Have you been following our meal plan?"

"For the most part."

"Good to hear."

"Lacey, can you give us any hints about your book?"

"Only that many lives were affected and with the release of my book, I'm hoping to right some wrongs." A car horn beeped. "That's my ride."

Susan and Mike began walking toward Evan's. "I can't wait to read that book of hers. I think it's directly related to Neil Schmidt's murder. *Double Jeopardy.* Sounds like it involves twin studies to me."

"Come on. You're still on that kick?"

"Now that Schmidt is dead, the book is free to be released. You heard her. She had several axes to grind, including the suicide of her sister. Neil Schmidt was on that roof with her and failed to stop it."

"That was years ago, right?"

"And what about the photos and files in her office?"

"What photos and files?"

"Never mind. Let's get going."

Chapter 17

"What's this, the third or fourth book signing we've been to in the past few weeks?" Valerie nudged closer, asserting her place in line."

"I can't wait to read this one. I'm sure we'll find some interesting answers. What's taking her so long? She was supposed to start an hour ago."

Valerie took off her coat. "It's too warm in here and I'm getting hungry."

"We can grab lunch afterwards." Susan unzipped her jacket. She was surprised at how many people were out in the middle of a Tuesday. She waved at Boston Talmich, hustling his way into the line next to Judith Potter. "He was sure in a hurry to get here. Valerie, keep my place in line."

She cut into the line ahead of them." Can't wait to read the new book. Nice that you both were able to come over and support your friend."

Boston looked at his phone. "If she doesn't get here soon, I'll have to leave. I have clinic hours." He looked back and forth at the door.

"Boston, you've got dirt on the back of your coat. Let me get it off for you."

He pulled away. "No, it's okay. I have a pile of dry cleaning to drop off at home anyway."

Another twenty minutes passed, before Lacey's publicist approached the crowd.

"I have some horrific news to relay. Lacey Daniels was hit by a car and died an hour ago." The publicist's voice cracked. She took a tissue from her purse. "We appreciate your support and together mourn the death not only of Lacey Daniels the author, but Lacey Daniels the dietician, Lacey Daniel's the seeker of truth, and Lacey Daniels, the person."

Someone in the crowd said, "Can we still buy the book?"

Susan was appalled at the insensitivity, but was wondering the same thing.

"The books are on sale. Barnes and Noble is setting up a display in the front of the store."

Valerie made her way over. "God rest her soul. I'm in shock."

Susan looked at Judith and Boston. Judith was sobbing, and Boston stood shaking his head.

"You must be shocked, too."

"Hit by a car? It doesn't make sense," said Judith. "She knows these streets inside and out."

Valerie said, "Maybe she was distracted, thinking about the book signing."

"Just when she was about to see her book change lives." Boston dabbed at his eyes. "It changed mine. I've got to get back to the hospital."

"Judith, do you know what's in that book?"

"I haven't read it. It was just released today."

"But you've made comments about Neil Schmidt's work. Is he part of the exposé?"

"No comment. Now, I'd better get back to work as well."

Valerie had ducked into a quiet corner with her phone. She came back and said, "Jazzy says Lacey was dead at the scene. A hit and run. So far, no witnesses."

"It had to be intentional, given the timing."

"And if it were accidental, you know the driver would have stopped and tried to help. I think we should get in that line. I'll grab two copies of Lacey's book."

While they waited to pay for the books, a steady stream of customers flooded the store. *Word sure travels fast. If her book wasn't destined to be a hit before, it sure will be now.* By the time she got back to the apartment, Evan was home. She heard the shower running.

Mike said, "Where on Earth were you all this time?"

"Turn on the news. Lacey Daniels was murdered."

"What? At the book signing?"

"No, before. A hit and run. I wonder if they have any suspects yet."

Evan, hair still wet from the shower, said, "Are you getting ready? We're going to dinner with Cara, did you forget?"

Susan *had* forgotten given the events of the day. "We'll be ready in a flash. Evan, what do you make of the hit and run?"

"Hit and run? I heard about it as I was leaving the hospital. I thought it was an accident."

"Valerie's daughter, Detective Lowe, hinted that it was intentional."

"The driver was probably talking on his phone, or texting."

"Don't you think he'd have stopped?"

"Not necessarily. Especially if he had been on the phone, or drunk, or a million other reasons. Get going so we're not late."

Susan knew Evan was wrong. It was too much of a coincidence, Lacey being hit the day her book gets released? Was the killer the same person who killed Neil Schmidt, or did Lacey kill Schmidt, and someone else murder her? Lacey killing Schmidt made sense given it freed up the book release. Who else was impacted by the release of the book?

"Mom, hurry up. I don't want to miss our reservation."

Susan ran the blow drier through her hair, and pulled on the dressier black stretch pants with the one dressy top she had packed. *These pants feel tighter than before. Must be Evan's dryer.*

"Mike, can you close this necklace for me?"

"I'll try." He fastened the silver locket around her neck.

"Mike, those pants are huge on you. Maybe you can wear the suit jacket you wore for Match Day so it won't be as noticeable." *Mike's losing weight, and I'm finding it. I have to watch the stress eating. Starting tomorrow.*

He put on the jacket, which had also gotten loose. "I hope I like Vietnamese food. I would have preferred Italian myself."

"Cara doesn't like Italian food. She has this thing about cheese."

Evan turned out the lights. "Let's go."

On the way out, Susan eyed the new book on the table, anxious to discover what secrets it revealed. Even if it meant staying up all night.

The restaurant was housed in an old mansion with a historical plaque at the door. Susan's stomach growled. She and Valerie had that early lunch and she hadn't eaten since.

"Cara, you look beautiful," said Susan. She had been waiting at the restaurant entrance. She wore a casual red dress with a denim jacket and tights. *What a gorgeous bride she'll be.*

"So do you. Hot pink is your color."

Mike said, "Evan tells us this is a busy rotation for you. We've hardly had a chance to visit."

"Fortunately, this rotation ends in a few days. By the way, you're looking well. How are you feeling?"

"I'm getting there. This is the first restaurant dinner since before the operation."

The hostess seated them next to a fountain. The tables were a little close together, but the place had atmosphere. They perused the menus.

"All these dishes have numbers, not names," said Susan.

Evan said, "That's how they do it in Vietnamese restaurants. The ingredients are listed, and if you have a question, they're very eager to help."

"That's one of the reasons I love this place. Of course, the food is out of this world," said Cara. "Evan says you were at the book signing this afternoon."

"The signing that never happened. I'm shocked at the timing of the accident."

"I was working in the ED when they brought her in. She was already dead, and by the looks of the muddy tire tracks on her, that car ran over her forwards and backwards. Someone wanted to be sure she didn't have a chance."

The waiter brought spring rolls to the table. Mike picked one up, inspected it, and proceeded to demolish it, to Susan's delight. They proceeded to order dinner.

"My friend's daughter is the detective investigating Dr. Schmidt's murder. This has to be related but I can't figure out how."

Mike said, "That's because you're not the detective. Can't we enjoy a pleasant dinner without talking about murders?"

"How are your parents doing, Cara?"

"Fine. Dad had to fly back right after the ceremony, but Mom spent a few days here with me and my sister. Actually, I should say with her granddaughter. That's the real draw. Ever since Trina was born, Mom's been making frequents visits."

Evan and Cara will have gorgeous children together. "Grandchildren are a blessing. I'm sure Evan has shown you pictures of his nieces, but in case he hasn't..." She pulled out her phone. "This is Annalise at her school Valentine's Day party, and here's me and Mia at story hour. It looks like there are a lot of things to do in St. Louis with kids."

"Aww... Annalise looks like you."

Susan felt her peacock pride surface. "Mia, of course, lacks the family resemblance, coming from China, but we have our own bond. We're both adopted."

"Really? I mean, Evan told me about Mia but I didn't realize you were also."

"Didn't know it myself until just a few years ago. It's a long story."

The waiter reappeared and set the food on the table. "Do you need anything else at the moment? Refills?"

"We're fine for now," said Mike. He twirled a rice noodle around his chopstick.

"You're the second person who I've heard recently discovered a family member later in life." Cara maneuvered the chop sticks like a pro.

"Really? Who else?" She tried unsuccessfully to get the chicken bite to her mouth.

"Boston Talmich."

"He surely knows he's adopted with those fair skinned parents of his." She tried stabbing the chopstick through the chicken, then shoveling the Chinese broccoli against the side of the plate. The broccoli fell into her napkin-protected lap.

"Yes, but he recently found his birth mother thanks to Lacey Daniels going through Dr. Schmidt's research. I heard Boston talking about it at a lunch lecture. I was sitting behind him and Judith Potter and he said Lacey Daniels found his birth mother *and* a twin brother he didn't know he had."

"So the hairdresser is his mother after all. A twin brother? Did the mother keep the twin and give him away? That's awful."

"No, the mother didn't know she'd given birth to twins. He was searching for the brother."

"Why did Dr. Schmidt have this information?"

"His research used identical twins raised separately. He was supposed to give full disclosure and have permission from both parents, but he fudged it. I think that's what Lacey Daniel's book is about."

Evan said, "How's your food, Mom?"

She grabbed her fork and took a bite. "Delicious."

Chapter 18

Susan stayed up all night reading Lacey's book. What an eye opener! Neil Schmidt spent his career looking to answer the old "nature vs. nurture" question. He worked with an adoption agency, finding the names of identical twins who were adopted separately. He was paying the agency not to tell prospective parents that a twin existed, in order to have subjects. The permission forms were forged.

"Susan, don't I have an appointment with Boston Talmich today?"

"Yes, thanks for reminding me. Want to go for a walk before I get in the shower?" She was exhausted, but committed to getting Mike strong again.

"I'll ride the exercise bike instead." She watched him rinse out his empty cereal bowl and put the skim milk back into the fridge. *Yes, we're making progress.*

After her shower, she turned on the news and immediately saw a story on Lacey's death. The reporter was now calling it a hit and run and asking for any witnesses to come forward. There was a teaser about a story to air later: *Twins kept apart, angry parents deceived...new book by dead author reveals all.* The camera zoomed in to the cover of the new book, the title, *Double Jeopardy*, flashed from bright to brighter, then went black.

She wondered how many parents and twins were affected. Lacey must have gotten permission to feature their accounts in her own book. Would any of those contacts have been angry at her? Angry enough to kill her? Why? Had someone changed their mind about their story being made public?

"Shouldn't we get to the hospital?"

"Yes, I'm ready. Zip up your jacket. Got your scarf?"

"Yes, Mom. It's supposed to be a high of 60 today so I think the scarf is overkill."

Mike was able to walk a little faster and breathe a little easier on the way to his appointment. Again, progress. During Mike's appointment, she sat in the waiting room, took out her phone, and caught up with her Facebook friends. *I need to get a pulse on how Boston felt about Lacey's revelations.*

When the door opened, she said, "How's he doing? We picked up the medication you prescribed."

"He'll be fine, right, Mr. Wiles?"

"I'm looking forward to getting home to Westbrook and my routine."

Susan said, "It's been anything but routine around here. Boston, I'm so sorry about your friend. I'd only just met her, but Lacey had a good heart. She truly wanted to help people through her work."

"She was a positive addition to the staff here at St. Agnes."

"You must have been shocked, learning you had a twin brother and finding your mom after all these years."

"Finding my birth mother has been great, though I already have the best parents on Earth. Lacey helped me track down my twin. I found out she had been in contact with him for a while but she pretended like she just found him."

"That must have made you mad."

"She lied to me. I thought she was on my side, but she was only interested in a scoop for her book."

"Did you find him yet?"

"I've got a lead." The waiting room door opened. "My next patient is here. I've got to get back to work."

Susan hooked her arm around Mike's waist. When they were out of earshot, she said, "At the book signing, Boston had dirt on the back of his coat and his hair was tussled. I wonder where he'd been at the time of Lacey's death."

"You think he ran over Lacey, then zoomed over to Barnes and Noble? And in what car, the one he'd just turned into a murder weapon?"

"Anything's possible. Want to get lunch? It's early, so we can walk over to the Green Deli and window shop along the way."

They passed a card store, a gourmet coffee shop where you could buy flavored coffee beans, and a children's clothing boutique.

"Look at that adorable dress with the cats on it. I have to get it for Annalise." She led Mike inside.

"If you're buying for Annalise, you have to get Mia something, too." He rifled through the rack of dresses. "Here's one for Mia. She loves ponies. Is this her size?"

"Looks about right. Here, I'll pay for it and we can go eat." She looked at the price tags. *I'll have to use my credit card. Hopefully Mike will be back to work by the time the bill comes.*

At the deli, Susan shared a spinach wrap with Mike. She ordered sweet potato fries to go along with it.

"Why didn't you get the regular fries? You know I hate sweet potatoes."

"I don't remember you ever tasting sweet potatoes. Try one."

"No thanks. I'll grab a cookie on the way out."

They finished in silence. Mike left most of his half of the spinach wrap on the plate.

"Aren't you hungry?"

"No. I'm getting tired. Can we head back?"

Susan finished what was on her plate. "Sure."

Back at Evan's apartment, Susan curled up with Lacey's book while Mike napped. She'd started reading *Double Jeopardy* last night, but had been too exhausted to get very far.

So where was I? Chapter Two. The twins used in the study were solicited by an adoption agency. The agency received kickbacks from Neil Schmidt for acquiring multiples from poor, young, mothers unable to raise their babies. The agency had contacts at various high schools and clinics around the city and offered extremely generous monetary compensation in exchange for their babies.

Susan could barely keep reading. *They scouted out pregnant, vulnerable teens and made them offers they couldn't refuse given their economic situations.* She had a flashback to what she'd learned about her own adoption and anger welled inside of her.

Keeping the fact that they were multiples a secret, the agency placed the subjects with similarly matched, upper class families. To make his study more scientific, the families chosen had parents of similar ages, who'd been married a similar number of years, and if they had other children, the sex and age spreads of the siblings in each placement were identical.

Mike stirred. "Whatcha reading?"

"Lacey's book. This is incredible. Teen mothers of multiples were paid to put their twins up for adoption."

"What are you talking about?"

"Schmidt had an adoption agency place the twins separately into similar family situations, so he could study them! The adoptive parents had no idea a twin existed."

"That's terrible."

"Then he visited the 'subjects' every six months to gather data on them. Like lab rats!"

"That accounts for those comments about Schmidt being unethical."

"Boston found out he has a twin, but the other 'subjects' must have been equally incensed when they found out what went on. Maybe they even blamed Lacey for not notifying them sooner."

"So they killed Schmidt, for an obvious reason, then took it out on Lacey for keeping it under her hat?"

"Books aren't written overnight. Or maybe they were embarrassed and didn't *want* the book released. They may have thought by killing Lacey before the big debut, the book release would be delayed. I'm just brainstorming."

"Are any names mentioned in the book?"

"She uses pseudonyms to protect their privacy, but from the details she gives, their identities may not be hard to uncover."

"So, who has Lacey's notes? Somewhere those subjects are identified. The police should check it out."

Evan came in with Wes.

"I left my fishing pole in my closet," said Wes.

"Did you take up fishing after the fire? I mean, with your leg and all...I'll bet you had to give up on sports..." She felt her face turning redder by the minute. "I mean..."

Wes chuckled. "It's okay. I've never been able to do sports." He turned his attention to Mike. "Mr. Wiles, you look better than last time I saw you. Your color is better and you don't look as worn out. Ever go fishing?"

"Not since I was about twelve."

"I'm glad to see you recovering so well."

"Slowly but surely. I hope we can go back home maybe as soon as next week."

"That's great. I'm sure you miss your own bed."

Susan said, "What do you make of Lacey Daniel's death? What a shock."

"Yeah, freaky timing. I heard she was on the way to a book signing or something."

"She was. I was at Barnes and Noble when her publicist made the announcement. I've been reading her book. She uncovered quite the scandal."

"I heard the nurses talking about it. I really liked Dr. Schmidt. It's hard to believe he did all those things."

"How did Lacey know? I mean, she blamed him for her sister's suicide, but how did she dig up the other stuff? She had to have gotten into his files."

"Wouldn't be the first time."

"What do you mean?"

"Nothing. She struck me as kind of...what's the word?"

"Nosy? Persistent?"

"Yeah, both of those. Let me get what I came for." He retrieved the racquet and left. After dinner, there was special extended coverage of Lacey's bombshell. The reporter interviewed a set of twins who had just found out the truth and claimed many more had been calling the station for information.

Mike said, "You know they weren't all Schmidt's lab rats. Once you throw something out like that, it gets every adoptee who hears about it wondering. And envisioning a rich payout from a lawsuit."

"You're so skeptical. Imagine learning something like that after all those years. They have to be angry."

Evan said, "Not to mention those who found out not quite as recently. If you're trying to link Lacey's death with Dr. Schmidt's, it had to be someone who found out before Match Day."

They continued watching the program. A man said, "Because of this debacle, I've lost my son. Those interviews over the years...the tests...I told that Dr.

Schmidt something was off with my boy, but he kept saying he was a normal boy, exhibiting normal rage and depression. I wanted to get him help, take him for therapy, but Dr. Schmidt talked us out of it. By the way, he destroyed my marriage along the way. Living with the constant rages, violence, and depression...my wife couldn't take anymore and left us."

"I'm so sorry for your loss. When did your son die?" The reporter moved in closer.

"He's not dead, though he might as well be. He's been in prison ever since he was convicted of road rage. He got cut off in traffic...would have cost him all of ten minutes getting to his amateur league hockey game, but instead, he ran the car off the road, and beat the poor man to death with his hockey stick."

"And you blame Dr. Schmidt?"

"If we'd gotten my son therapy, medication...his mental illness would have been under control. Instead, he's sitting in a jail cell. I thought he was the professional. We took his ill-given advice."

Susan said, "If anyone has motive..."

Evan answered, "What was the trigger? And why go after Lacey?"

Mike said, "Lacey knew about Schmidt for some time before the book came out. If I were that father and I found out how long she'd sat on this, I'd be angry, too."

On the screen, the father said, "He found his twin, you know. Rather, his twin found him, out of the blue. The day before the incident occurred. The day before! My son couldn't cope with it, not like that, especially given his condition. Had this author warned us earlier we could have prepared him."

"There's your answer," said Mike.

Susan picked up her phone.

"Who are you calling?"

"Valerie, It's Susan. Did you watch the interview?"

"Yes. I tried calling Jazzy but couldn't reach her. She took Elijah on a Cub Scout camping trip for a few days. School's on spring break. Can't even call her. I did a little search while I was watching. The man owns a restaurant near the university."

"Interesting. Sounds like it could be our man."

Mike motioned for her to get off the phone. "Val, I've gotta go. We'll talk tomorrow."

As soon as she hung up, both Mike and Evan said in unison, "Stay out of it."

"But Detective Lowe is out of town, and I want to see this case solved before we go back home."

"Mom, it's not your business. It can wait a few more days."

"Besides," added Mike, "if you think the man has committed two homicides, why would you go within ten miles of him? I thought you'd become better about that over the years."

"It's not like I'm going to go chase after him myself. I was just going to…"

"Mom, Dad's right. It can wait a few days until Detective Lowe returns. Now, don't get Dad upset. It's bad for his heart." He gave her a stern look, the way he did when she asked him about marrying Cara.

"Okay, okay. I'll stay out of it."

Chapter 19

The next morning, Mike was scheduled for tests at the hospital. Given a favorable progress report, they'd be able to travel home.

"It'll be a few hours," said the nurse. "You can wait, or I can call you when he's finished if you leave me your cell number."

She wasn't sure where she'd go, but just in case, Susan took the latter option. She kissed Mike on the cheek. "Hope you pass!"

"Me too. I miss the girls."

It was too early for lunch, so she headed to the waiting room. On the way, she ran into Boston.

"Mrs. Wiles, I'm not seeing Mike today, am I?"

"No, he's here for follow-up tests. We're hoping he'll be given the all clear to travel."

"That's great. He should continue his sessions when he goes back home. Do you want me to refer you to someone?"

"Thanks, sure. By the way, did you watch that story on channel 10 last night?"

"No, I was working."

"It broke the whole illegal testing story. A man was interviewed whose son committed suicide over it. Can you imagine?"

"I can. It's a serious matter. I know the upheaval I've been through because of it."

"You worked with Dr. Schmidt. Didn't you know about these studies?"

"They weren't current. By the time I came along, he was on a completely different topic."

"But you said at the reception it was top secret."

"No, Evan said that. All research involving human test subjects is considered confidential. If details get out, it can ruin lives, as you see now."

"Have you contacted your twin brother?"

"We've arranged to meet for dinner. I'm excited, and a bit nervous. I imagine it'll be like looking in a mirror."

"Better late than never, right? I discovered I had a brother, George, not long after finding my own birth mother."

"Are you close now?"

"He lives in Florida, near my birth mother. I wouldn't say we're close, but we keep in touch. I'm glad we connected."

He looked at his watch. "I've gotta go. Hope Mike's tests turn out okay."

"Good luck with your brother."

After he left, she took a walk outside. Valerie called.

"Are you free for lunch? I was thinking of this new place I heard about. Near the university."

"I'm in. Can you pick me up? Mike's having tests at the hospital, he'll be a few hours."

"You bet."

Susan waited outside the hospital. She hoped Mike would be given the all clear to travel so they'd be able to go back home. She wasn't feeling all that well lately herself. Her blood sugars, when she remembered to check, were running high. *I have an endocrinologist appointment in a few weeks. I'll have to get things under control by then.* She did the calculations in her head. *Let's see, the A1C will measure my average blood sugar over three months. I have a month left to pull down the numbers and make the average work out.* She spotted Valerie's red Nissan.

Valerie's car was a mess. In the back, toy soldiers and a Nerf football. In the front, a Dunkin Donuts coffee cup in the drink holder, and a crumpled Egg Mc Muffin wrapper on the floor of the passenger side. She could still smell the grease.

"Ready to try some St. Louis chili at *Casa Joe*? I read a review on *Yelp*. It's very popular with the college kids."

"How do you know he'll be there?"

"It said in the review the owner is on the premises during lunch every weekday."

"Have you heard from your daughter?"

"No. Didn't expect to. They're out in the woods at the Cub Scout camp. Supposed to be all rustic like. They were told not to bring anything electronic."

College students weren't hard to spot. Susan noted the comeback of Birkenstock sandals and long skirts as she watched the girls pass. "Hey, look. That girl's running around in tights with her midriff showing. No coat. She must be freezing."

"Unless she actually was running, or came from the gym down the block. Come on. The restaurant is right here and I found myself street parking. Easy peasy."

The restaurant was sandwiched between a pet bakery and a Starbucks. There were a few tables outside, but you had to order inside at the counter in any case. Susan struggled to read the menu on the wall behind the counter.

"What are you getting?"

Valerie said, "The *Cha Cha Cha Chili*. And a side salad."

Susan debated between the *Aye Carumba*, and the *Spirit of St. Chili*. After a chat with the counter person, she said, "I'm not going to tax my stomach today. I'm going for the *Spirit of St. Chili*."

They sat at a brightly painted wooden table with a chair that Susan couldn't quite get to stop rocking back and forth whenever she shifted her weight. They stuck the plastic number on the table as instructed, and drank their sodas.

"I don't see the owner, do you?" asked Susan.

"Not yet, but we're early for lunch. He'll be here."

"Should we tell him we saw him on TV and that we're friends of Lacey's?"

"Let's play it by ear. What time is your husband finished?"

"I sent him a text and he hasn't answered, which means he's hooked up to wires or inside some medical machine. We won't linger. I don't want him to have to wait."

A young lady in a tight t-shirt with the restaurant logo on the front brought their orders to the table in red plastic baskets. "Enjoy."

Susan took a bite, then gulped her water. "Glad I went for mild. I hate to imagine how hot the spicy dishes are."

"I like a little spice," said Valerie. She pointed out the male server in the even tighter t-shirt. "Yum yum." Turning her head toward the kitchen, she said, "Hey, that's our guy. The one with the moustache. I recognize him from the picture on the website, though he's not wearing the poncho and straw hat. He's coming toward our table."

"Good afternoon, ladies. Are you enjoying the food?" He had leathery skin, as though he'd spent years working out in the sun. *Younger than Val or me, but not by too much.* He was thinner in person than he had looked on television.

"Delicioso," said Susan. "This place is hopping. Have you been in business long?"

"A couple of years. Retired early from the construction business to live my dream, as they say. When my father died, I used my inheritance to buy this place. Joe was my father, thus the name."

"I think I saw you on TV last night."

"Unfortunately, yes. Having a twin brother materialize out of thin air? Life is full of surprises."

"I went through the same thing, you know. I found my birth parents, and a brother not that long ago."

"Really? Was your brother in jail like mine is?"

Susan felt awful. How could she be so insensitive. "No, not even close." Her brother, George, worked for the DEA.

Valerie said, "How did that doctor get away with it? Good thing Lacey Daniels exposed him or you may have never known you had a brother. Did you know before the book was released?"

"Yeah. She came by and broke the news. Gave me contact information and everything. I just wish she'd done it sooner."

"I'll bet you didn't shed tears over the doctor's death, or the author's either."

"I was furious at Doctor No Good, but not so much at Lacey Daniels. After all, she did expose this whole scandal, for better or worse."

Valerie said, "He crossed someone enough to get himself murdered."

"Murdered? I thought he had a heart attack or something. I came back from visiting my son in New Hampshire and I saw it on the news but they didn't mention murder."

"Yeah, they're still looking for suspects."

"I better keep circulating." He reached into his apron pocket. "Here's a coupon for next time. Hope to see you back here soon."

Susan scooped up the remainder of her chili with a tortilla chip. "I don't think he's guilty, do you?"

"Not at all. At least we found a new lunch spot. Guess we should get you back to your hubby."

Valerie dropped her off in front of the hospital. "Call me later and let me know how he did."

Susan went to the cardiologist's waiting room. Wes came by and said, "They just finished up."

"Was everything okay?"

"One of the tests showed an irregularity. They want to redo it next week."

"So he can't travel?"

"Not yet. Better to be sure, right?"

She felt her heart sink. "Yeah. Is he ready to go?"

"Come on back." Mike was sitting in the exam room.

"I've been doing everything they told me to do. Why can't I go home?"

"We just want to be sure. It happens sometimes. In another week chances are everything will be fine."

"Guess you're not getting your room back yet."

"I don't mind. With my schedule, Bethany and I hardly see each other. I'll come by for my suit later. I'm interviewing with a pharmaceutical company."

"But I thought you were starting your cardiology residency next year?"

"I got my last choice. Do I really want to move out to North Dakota for the next five years? I'm just weighing my options."

Susan grabbed Mike's jacket and led him by the elbow.

"Stop, I'm not an invalid. I can walk on my own."

"I texted Evan. He brought the car over."

"Yesterday, I was fine to go walking around the park, but today I can't make the short walk back to Evan's apartment? I'm sick of this whole thing. Let's just book the ticket anyway. What do they know?"

"And if you collapse on the plane? We can wait one more week."

Chapter 20

When they got back to Evan's, Mike planted himself in the recliner and was snoring within minutes. Evan whirred together protein powder and bananas in the Ninja.

"Tell me the truth. Is he ever going to fully recover?"

"Of course, he will. This is a minor setback, that's all." He snapped a lid on his shake. "I'm going to run over to the gym in a bit."

"What's Cara up to? Is she working?"

"I think so."

"You don't know her schedule? You and Cara have been together since the day you started med school, and even decided to match together. What's keeping you from making a commitment to her?"

"I just have to be sure. How do I know there isn't an even better match out there for me? And being married to another doctor will mean neither of us is ever home."

"Do you love her?"

"Well, yes. But I have loans to repay, and so does she. I don't have money to buy a ring, and besides, I know nothing about diamonds, nor do I have time to do the research."

"Look, you have been super logical since the day you were born, but sometimes, you have to trust your heart. Ask yourself how you'd feel if she wasn't in your life."

He cupped his hand around his ear. "I can't hear it."

"Hear what?"

"The melancholy violin music."

She swatted him with the dish towel. "You should listen to your mother."

"I've gotta get to the gym. I'll be home for dinner."

She called after him, "You don't have to get married tomorrow. Engagements can last years." She heard the door slam.

She wasn't trying to rush him into marriage. She just wanted to be sure he didn't let someone he loved slip out from under his fingers while he wasn't paying attention. Both Lynette and Evan were far more logical and less emotional than either of their parents. *Maybe they inherited their grandmother Audrey's genes.*

She went into the guest room, and was struck by the mess it had become. She'd seen a suit wrapped in dry cleaning plastic hanging in the closet. *I'll bring it into the living room so Wes doesn't see the pile of newspapers on the floor and my clothes airing out over his desk chair.* When she went to pull it out, a box fell from the shelf. She scooped up the contents.

Photos of Wes with his mother and brother. A yearbook. A running medal. A college transcript, a class ring …

"Susan, where are you? I need water."

"I'll be right there."

She scooped the papers back into the box and brought Mike a glass of water.

"Want to go for a walk?"

"No. I'm tired."

"But you just had a nap."

"Leave me alone." He closed his eyes.

"Are you sleeping again? Really?"

Still unable to figure out the remote, she pulled out the book she'd been reading. When the doorbell rang, she tried to wake Mike, but he wouldn't open his eyes.

At the door, Wes was standing next to a slender woman with auburn hair.

"Mrs. Wiles, this is my mother, Amy. She's visiting for a few days."

"Hi, how nice to meet you. I'm Susan, Evan's mom." Embarrassed, she said, "And sleeping in the recliner, is my husband Mike, Evan's dad. He had heart surgery so he gets very tired at times."

"Yes, Wes filled me in. If he had to have heart surgery, this is the place to be. Wes was hoping to do his cardiology residency here."

"Do you work in the medical field?"

"I guess you could say that. I work in medical records."

"North Dakota is supposed to be beautiful." What else could she say? *I'm sorry your son got his last choice of residency and will be stuck in the boonies. Remind him to bring his snow boots?* Her eyes lingered on Amy's hand.

"My hand was badly burned in the house fire. My whole arm, in fact. I was trying to pull my son out."

"I'm so sorry. Evan told me you lost a son."

"I don't feel like I'll ever get past it. Thank God Wes survived." She fingered a gold locket hanging from her neck.

An awkward silence followed. Susan's eyes teared up just imagining how it would feel to lose a child. "I've got your suit right here, Wes. This is the one you meant, right?"

"Yes, thanks."

"Wes, before you go, how worried should I be about Mike? We expected him to get a clean bill of health."

"It could have been a glitch with the test. Everything else checked out. Better to err on the side of caution." He patted his pockets. "Oops, forgot something." He headed back into his bedroom. After a few minutes, he returned holding a small white box in his palm.

"Good luck on your interview. Nice to meet you, Amy."

After they left, she poked Mike. "Wake up. That was embarrassing, you snoring away while we had company."

"What company?"

"Wes and his mother. Never mind. Go back to sleep."

She went into the bedroom and changed the sheets. Fixing the dust ruffle, she noticed something on the floor. *This must have fallen out of the box.* It was a Social Security Card. She looked at the name. *Jake Jacobs. He saved his brother's Social Security Card as a memento.* She tucked it back in the box along with the other items, wiping a tear with her sleeve.

Mike had fallen back to sleep. Annoyed at his retreat into depression, and determined to keep her own health problems in check, she threw on her coat and grabbed Evan's spare key. She'd take a walk around the block to Whole Foods, or go over to Forest Park. She deliberately slammed the door on her way out.

Outside the building, Boston was on his phone, so deep in conversation that he didn't notice her. She froze and listened.

"Now? I thought we were meeting tonight? Urgent? I'll be there in a few." Boston stuck the phone back in his pocket. Instead of getting in his car, like she expected, Boston went through the gate and headed toward the park. He walked quickly and focused straight ahead. Susan decided to opt for the park route herself.

She was feeling winded by the time they got to the crosswalk. She stayed just behind him, not that she was overly worried. She'd simply say she was taking a walk in the park if he questioned her. Focused on not getting too far behind, she narrowly missed being struck by a bike that crossed her path with inches to spare.

Where's he going? We're almost at the art museum. Now he has his phone out again.

After a short rest on the museum steps, Boston headed in the direction of the boats. It was still too chilly for water sports, but Boston made his way to the water's edge. The boat dock was abandoned, except for a man in a puffer vest facing the water. Susan followed Boston as he approached the man, then hid behind the boat house, still within earshot. Boston made the first move.

"So we finally meet."

"Sorry, it can't be more ceremonious, but this is urgent."

Susan scooted around the corner for a closer look. He sounded just like Boston.

"I'm Preston Monahan."

When he turned around to shake Boston's hand, she realized who he was meeting. *It's Boston's twin. They're identical except for the beard.*

"Boston Talmich. I've always wondered what I'd look like if I grew a beard."

Preston laughed a tense laugh. "This is just weird."

"Finding out in your thirties you have a twin?"

"Finding out you have a twin and then learning that's the tip of the iceberg."

"What do you mean? You've talked to our birth mother, right?"

"Yes, we met over coffee. There's more."

"Tell me. Nothing will surprise me at this point."

"I'd rather show you. When do you get off work?"

"I have clinic hours this afternoon. My last appointment is at 7:00."

"Meet me at Delmar Cemetery tonight at eight. I've got to get back to work. Give me your phone, I'll put in the address."

"You can't tell me what this is about?"

"You'll want to see for yourself."

She stayed behind the boathouse until both brothers went their separate ways, then sat on a bench and called Valerie.

"Can you meet me at Delmar Cemetery tonight at eight? Yes. Outside. Got it. Text me when you get there. Thanks."

Chapter 21

Valerie offered to pick her up and was waiting in front of Evan's building later that evening. Susan told Evan and Mike they were going to a movie together. She slid into the car, tossing a McDonald's bag off the passenger seat and onto the floor.

"So what's this all about? You can't keep me in suspense like this."

"I don't know any more myself."

"Why did he want to meet him at night, when it's dark and creepy? I don't like cemeteries even by day. You got your mace?"

"They both work by day. Do you know how to get there?"

"Yeah. Went to a funeral there last year."

They drove past the park, onto the highway. It was the tail end of rush hour, and after a few delays, they exited onto a dark road. Valerie said, "I don't like this. We could be falling right into a trap."

"They don't know we're here. If anyone is falling into a trap, it will be Boston. Is your daughter back in town?"

"Not till tomorrow, but we can still call the station."

"And say what? A nosy old lady was eavesdropping and got her friend to help tail a doctor to the cemetery. At night."

"I'm gonna dial up 911 and keep my hand on the phone just in case."

The windy road snaked up a hill lined with pine trees. Sporadic rain drops dinged the windshield. The paved road morphed into a dirt road, and ended at an iron gate.

"It's locked. How are we supposed to get in?"

"If we walk, we can go around it. Let's park behind those trees."

"I don't see any other cars. Think they're going to show up?"

"It's not eight yet. Come on. We'll wait behind the bushes." The cemetery smelled like a Christmas tree lot, the aroma enhanced by the light rain which fell steadily. She fingered the mace in her jacket pocket. They held still, then...

Valerie screamed. "What's that?"

"Shh." Susan's heart jumped. She looked toward the sky. "It's just an owl."

"Sound more like a coyote."

"Whatever it was, it's quiet now."

The trees rustled. "Did you see that?"

Susan looked up and bravely said, "It's just bats." *I hope they don't have rabies. I hear the shots hurt terribly.*

"Do you think the brother is a murderer? Is he going to show Boston the bodies he was responsible for?"

"Valerie, keep that imagination of yours in check."

"You're kidding right? Look who's calling the kettle black."

The bushes rustled. Susan held her breath, grabbing Valerie's arm. She whispered, "That's the brother, Preston, the one with the beard." More rustling. "And there's Boston. Come on."

Darting from tree to tree for cover, they followed the twin brothers through the cemetery.

Valerie whispered, "They're stopping in front of that tombstone."

The wind stirred the leaves into a miniature funnel cloud. Susan strained to hear the conversation. The twin spoke first, his words piercing the silence like a bullet.

"This was our brother. Read it. Jayson Parker. Died last year. Check out the birthday." He rubbed his glove across the inscription on the tombstone.

"Just because we share a birthday…"

"I looked up the obituary. And check out the photo in the frame over there."

"He looks like us."

Rain drops pelted the top of Susan's head.

"We were triplets. In the obituary, it said he died from a drug overdose. I did some research. His adoptive parents died in a car crash when he was eleven. Then he went in and out of foster care."

"How do you know this?"

"That author, Lacey Daniels, contacted me while doing research for her book. She had medical records and told me I had not one, but two brothers. Triplets."

"What a bombshell. I've barely come to terms with having a twin."

"I found out that doctor, Neil Schmidt, had set this up. That's why the author approached me. I went and had it out with him."

"With Dr. Schmidt?"

"Yeah. Pompous Jerk. Said this was all for the sake of science and the betterment of society. Sounded like Hitler. Scary stuff." Lightening flashed across the sky.

"I'd have punched him in the face."

"Well, I went one better than that."

A clap of thunder. The sky burst open.

"What did you do?" asked Boston. The sky lit up. The rain poured like buckets dumped from the heavens.

Preston pulled up his collar, put his arm around Boston, and they ran for their cars.

Soaked head to toe, Susan said, "Should we follow them?"

"Are you crazy? Let's get home before we both catch pneumonia."

When Susan walked into the apartment, Evan and Mike were watching TV. Mike said, "What'd you do, go to a drive-in and stand outside the car to watch the movie?"

"We had to park a mile away and when we got out of the theater, it was pouring."

"How was it?" said Evan.

"How was what?"

"The movie. What did you see?"

"Um, some spy thing. Very suspenseful. Lots of twists and turns. I've got to get out of these clothes." She ran into the bedroom. *And now for the sequel...*

Chapter 22

The next day, Evan was off.

"Mom, Dad and I are going to take a ride to the sporting goods store. Want to come?"

"No, thanks. Have some one-on-one time with your father."

Susan couldn't wait until they left, and immediately called Valerie.

"Where do we go from here? Is your daughter back yet?"

"They get home late tonight. We need to connect the dots. Boston finds out he's a twin, and his birth mother comes out of the woodwork. She gave away her baby after giving birth as a teenager and being wooed by a shady adoption agency—Neil Schmidt's pipeline for research subjects. Surprise? Shock is more like it. Given this chain of events, another brother dies. Bam. Boston has motive to kill Schmidt."

"And don't forget that day at the book signing. He had dirt all over his coat and he came in late—right before they made the announcement about Lacey's death. And he has access to drugs since he's a resident." She poured fresh water into Mittens' bowl while talking.

"I think this twin, Preston, has even greater motive. He knew about the scam longer, admits to going after Schmidt, though unclear about the details, and blames Lacey for not telling him they were triplets."

"The third brother drew the short straw, lost his adoptive parents, and wound up in the foster care system. Eventually, he got hooked on drugs and overdosed. Do we have enough to present to your daughter tonight?"

"We need hard evidence. Like a mark on Boston's car from where he hit Lacey, or a witness placing Preston with Schmidt around the time of the murder."

A mark on the car... Susan looked out the window. "Boston's car is in the parking lot. Hang on. I'll check it out." She took the phone with her, down the elevator, and outside.

"See anything?"

"Hang on." She walked around the car, bent down to look at the tires, and checked the front for dents or anything else hinting at having run someone over. "No, there's mud on the tires, but that's from last night. Nothing else suspicious." As she stood up, she felt someone behind her.

"Mrs. Wiles? What are you doing checking out my car?"

Her heart skipped a beat. She left the phone on, but tucked it in her pocket. "I was just...I lost my necklace. The one Mike got me for my birthday last year. I thought I might have dropped it out here. You didn't find it in your car, did you? From when you brought me home after the funeral?"

"No, but here." He unlocked his car. "We can have a look." He opened the front doors and poked his head in. "Check the back. It may have fallen under the seat."

Susan's knees ached as she bent under the back seat, reaching around as if she'd find this necklace she'd just fabricated. She found a few balled up receipts under there and instinctively stuck them in her pocket. "I don't see it."

"Well, I'll be on the lookout for it." He checked his Apple watch. "I've got to get going."

She went back inside, taking the phone from her pocket.

"Susan, are you still there?"

She got into the elevator. "Yeah. That was a close one."

"Ever think of doing improv? You're amazing on your feet."

"Well, if the sleuthing starts to bore me, maybe. Let me get inside, hang on a minute."

"So you didn't find anything suspicious, right?"

"No, but I grabbed some receipts off the car floor. It was a hunch." She unwrinkled them and laid them on the table. "There's a restaurant receipt, from yesterday. Here's one from Starbuck's. Let me figure out when this was." She took out her pocket calendar. "This is time stamped, from a Starbuck's on Martin Luther King Avenue. It's the same date as the book signing. And the time is right around when she was struck by the car!"

"Hold your horses. The Starbuck's on Martin Luther King Avenue is clear across town. It'd have taken him at least thirty minutes to get from there to the bookstore."

"Is it near where Lacey was hit?"

"Opposite end of town. I'd say it's an alibi, clearing him of Lacey's murder."

"He bought two coffees, exactly the same. Hazelnut Grandes."

"They have security cameras at these places. If need be, Jazzy can check and find out who he was with, if it matters."

"Good to know. I'd better go. Mike and Evan will be home any minute."

She thought about spending some time on the exercise bike. When she went into the guestroom, she wondered if a tornado had gone through when she wasn't looking. Her clothes were strewn everywhere, and the sheets hadn't been changed since they arrived. She gathered up the laundry, then stripped the bed.

She picked up something shiny from under the bed. An earring. A diamond stud. Identical to the one she'd found in Lacey's office the night she and Valerie broke in.

"Mom, are you here?"

"I'm in the bedroom." She took the earring with her. "Does Wes wear earrings?"

"He has a pierced ear. Sometimes he wears one."

She handed him the earring. "I found it when I was straightening up."

"Okay. I'll save it for him. Look what Dad bought."

Mike opened the bag he'd been holding and took out a pair of running shoes. "They've got little reflectors on them so we can walk after dark."

Susan was thrilled that he'd taken a positive step, so to speak. "They look so comfy, and they match your eyes!"

"I'll be running a marathon in no time."

Running a marathon. Track ribbon…bum leg…

"Evan, I saw a track ribbon in Wes's room. It must have been hard for him, not being able to run after the fire."

"What do you mean?"

"His leg was burned in the fire, right?"

"No, he was born with his leg like that. It had nothing to do with the fire."

"How'd he manage to be a high school track star?"

"He wasn't. If he's on his feet too long, he complains his leg aches. Dad and I are going to try out his new shoes. Want to come?"

"No, I think I'll pass."

After they left, Valerie called. "I told Jazzy about the receipts and they checked the security cameras outside the Starbuck's on Martin Luther King Drive. Both

Boston and his brother Preston were caught on camera at the time Lacey was struck by the car across town. They're both in the clear."

"Great. I'm working on a new lead. I'll call you back."

She went into Wes's room and took down the box from the closet shelf. She looked at the ribbon. First place in the mile run. Then she checked the transcripts. Straight A's. *Evan said Wes struggled with book work, but he had a stellar college transcript. Wes and his mother were both in the fire. His mother's arm was badly scarred as a result.* She remembered noticing Wes's long freckled fingers and snow white hands. No scars. *Did Wes also have a twin?*

She tried calling Valerie, but it went to voicemail. She put on her shoes and jacket, then headed to the hospital. *Boston Talmich had access to Dr. Schmidt's records.*

She took the elevator up to the psych clinic. "Is Dr. Talmich available?"

"He's with a patient."

"I'll wait." She sat down, got up, paced, sat back down. Finally, Boston escorted a patient out the office door.

"Boston? Can I speak to you?"

"You sound upset. Is your husband okay?"

"It's not that. I think I know who killed Dr. Schmidt, but I need your help."

"Shouldn't you be talking to the police?"

"Not without proof. Can you access Dr. Schmidt's records?"

"Yes, but it's unethical to do so if it isn't related to his research."

"It may be related."

"Well, I have an hour before my next patient. Follow me."

He led her to the psych lab, and into Dr. Schmidt's office. He flicked on the lights. "They took his laptop and most of the files, but I have access to the data base. I just need the code." He rummaged through the rolodex on Dr. Schmidt's desk. "Here it is."

He pulled a laptop from the locked closet. "My research computer...I stash it in here." He turned it on and waited. "What are you looking for?"

"I think Wes Jacobs had a twin and Dr. Schmidt was experimenting on them like he did with you and your brother."

"Here's the data base. Wes Jacobs." He clicked several keys. "I don't see him in here. He wasn't one of Dr. Schmidt's subjects."

"Are you sure?"

"Yes. I'm sure."

"Can we access birth certificates?"

"No, I have no way of doing that. It's probably illegal. I need to get back. Sorry I wasn't more help."

"Thanks for trying." *Back to the drawing board. Cara went to school with Wes, didn't she?* Somewhere she had Cara's mother's phone number...

Chapter 23

Found it. She sat outside the hospital and made a call. "This is Evan's mother, Susan. How are you doing?"

"Susan Wiles? Are the kids okay? Did something happen to Cara or Evan?"

"No, that's not why I called. At the reception, you said Wes Jacobs went to school with Cara, right?"

"That's right."

"And she and your son knew his brother, right? The one who was killed in the fire."

"Jake. He was a year younger than Wes. Why?"

"He didn't have a twin that you know of, did he?"

"It was just Wes and Jake as far as I know. Then Jake died in that awful fire. Why do you ask?"

Susan barged on. "Was Wes's brother a good student? I know that sounds strange…"

"Wes was first in his class. Scholar athlete. Beat out Cara for Valedictorian. The brother on the other hand…Jake was a disaster. Got arrested for shoplifting and I think he was mixed up in drugs. I don't think he ever graduated high school."

"Wes was a scholar athlete?"

He and my son were on the track team together. Wes and Travis both made all state the same year."

"Thanks for your help. Hope to be seeing you soon. One more question."

"Shoot."

"Hypothetically, what color would you lean towards if you were the mother of the bride?"

After she hung up, she tried Valerie again. Still voicemail. She was probably doing something over at Elijah's school, or else she had a doctor's appointment. She had said she was seeing a cardiologist.

The earring. She found the matching one on Lacey's floor the night they were locked in. It wasn't Lacey's after all, it belonged to Wes. He had to have been the one who clobbered them and stole the files, but why?

Birth certificates. How could she access them and see if Jake and Wes were actually twins? Wes's mother worked in medical records…

Just as she was about to walk back, she turned and was face to face with Wes.

She jumped. "Wes. I didn't see you coming."

"Is everything alright?"

"Um, yes, of course. Mike is out for a walk with Evan."

"Great to hear he's exercising. I'll bet the next round of tests will be completely fine and you'll be able to get home to New York."

"I'm hoping so. Oh, by the way I found your earring when I was straightening up the room. It had fallen under the bed."

"The diamond stud? Great. I thought I'd lost them for good. Are you sure you're okay?"

"Absolutely. I'd better get going. Maybe I'll catch up with Evan and Mike on the way home."

On the way back to Evan's, she tried Valerie once again. "Valerie? Where have you been?"

"I was doing a little shopping. You okay?"

"Can Jazmin check on something? I think Wes had a twin brother and that gave him motive to kill Neil Schmidt. He must have found out about it recently. Can your daughter check and see if Jake and Wes Jacobs have the same birthday?"

"How does that make sense? If they were growing up as brothers, why would he resent Neil Schmidt? And his mother obviously knew if they were twins."

"You're right. I can't fit all the pieces together yet, but I think I'm on the right track. Can you please ask Jazzy to check?"

"I'll ask, but no guarantees."

She reached Evan's building at the same time Mike and Evan did.

"Mom, are you okay? You're out of breath."

"No, I'm fine. How was the walk? Mike, your cheeks have some color back in them."

"Color? I think it's wind burn, but nevertheless, we had a good time."

Evan pushed the elevator button. "It's really windy out. I heard something about possible tornadoes this morning on the news."

"Don't those generally happen in the summer?" said Mike.

"They had a bad one several years ago in March. I've never seen one." Evan unlocked the door and Mittens came running to him, tail close to the floor.

"See, she hates me," said Susan. "Check out the body language."

"Don't be silly." Evan scooped her up. "Dad, I'll get you some water. It's important that you stay hydrated."

Susan's phone rang. "Valerie, what have you got?" She walked into the bedroom, closing the door behind her.

"Jazzy was annoyed that I'm still butting into her case, but to 'shut me up,' she looked into the birthdays. Jake and Wes Jacobs were not born on the same day. They were born in different months, and almost two years apart."

"Then, did Wes have a twin elsewhere?"

"Jazzy said he was a single birth. And to mind my own business. Told me to relay the message to you as well."

"I was sure Wes and Jake were twins. Back to the drawing board. Wes had no motive to kill Neil Schmidt or Lacey if he wasn't a research subject."

"We're running out of suspects. Hey, do you hear the wind over by you? I turned on the TV and they say there's a tornado watch. Stay safe."

"You too." She went back into the living room.

"Mom, the hospital just called. They found something in Dad's test results and asked me to bring him over ASAP so they can recheck something."

"Oh, my God. What do you think is wrong?"

"I'm going to bring him over right now."

"I'll come with you."

"No, stay here. It looks like a storm's brewing and you'll just be sitting in the waiting room. It could be nothing. We'll come right back."

Now what? Just when I thought Mike was getting back to his old self, another road block. The panic started with her heart ramping up, then her neck tensed and her head began to hurt. She tried to read, but couldn't focus. Mittens hid under the sofa the moment Evan left.

Her phone rang. *Did they find something already?*

"Susan, it's me. Jazzy called with one more bit of information. There was a death certificate filed for Jake Jacobs. He did die in that fire."

"Well, that seals the deal. Valerie?" The service went dead. "Valerie?" She tried calling back, but the call failed. The blinds rattled, in spite of the closed window. The lights flickered on and off. She tried calling Evan. Again, no service.

She heard what sounded like a train in the distance. Then, the key in the door. "Wes? Did you forget something you needed?"

He locked the door behind him, latching the chain as well. "I forgot to take care of something. A loose end."

The lights flickered. The train sound picked up both volume and speed. Susan saw a look in Wes's eyes that she'd never seen before.

"They said there was a tornado warning. It sounds bad out there." *He thinks the tornado is going to hit us. I see it in his face.*

"Yeah. If a tornado hits, anyone might get trapped under falling debris, hit her head, and turn up dead. Convenient, huh?"

"What are you talking about?"

"I know you accessed Dr. Schmidt's data base, and you found my earring. The match to the one I lost in Lacey's office the night I caught you and Ethyl Mertz sneaking around in there."

"That was you who knocked us out? Why?"

"Don't play stupid. I know you figured it out."

"Figured what out?"

He took a step toward her. "I can't leave any loose ends."

"For a while, I thought you and your brother were caught up in the whole twin study scam and you had motive, but now I know it isn't true. I know you and Jake were not twins, and there's a death certificate for Jake."

"Clever, right? Mom works in the medical records department. It was an easy switch."

"What switch?"

"Don't play dumb. When Wes was killed in the fire, Mom switched the records. She made it look like I had died. Made sense. I'm the one who had a criminal record and failed out of high school."

"But you made it this far through medical school."

"Never would have gotten into med school without using Wes's transcripts and credentials. It wasn't easy staying afloat."

"But you did. You were brilliant enough to get through."

"Hah. So brilliant I've been exiled to North Dakota? Better than being in jail, though. I'm not going back to jail."

The wind whipped, the train sounded louder and louder. "Are you saying you killed Dr. Schmidt? And Lacey? But why?"

She could barely hear the answer over the wind. "Schmidt went through birth records looking for twins to study. He somehow happened upon *my* records and figured out that Jake and I switched identities. He was going to have me thrown out of med school."

"You had access to heart meds."

"Yep. A little digitalis injected into the nicotine gum and there you have it. Didn't expect the dramatic exit during the reception, but it was a fitting end."

"But you killed Lacey Daniel's, too. Why her?"

"She went digging through Schmidt's records and found the switch. She was going to expose me. I couldn't let her do it."

The sound from outside was deafening. "I'm taking Mike back to Westbrook as soon as he gets the all clear. You don't have to worry about me."

He pulled a knife from the kitchen drawer. "I know I won't."

Susan felt the adrenaline coursing through her body. Fight or flight? Should she make a run for it, or pick up a chair and swing it at him? She ran for the door. The lights flickered. When she grabbed the handle, she realized the chain was on. She reached to unhook it just as the lights went out.

"Mrs. Wiles, you're not getting out of here."

Her heart pounded. It was pitch black inside. The window crashed in. Susan felt glass shards hit her arm and she ducked under the table. She couldn't see anything.

"I see you." Wes had a flashlight on his phone and was shining it at her. She scrambled out from under the table. Debris flew everywhere. She scrambled into the bathroom and locked the door. At least there were no windows in there. Wes pounded on the door.

"Open up. I'm getting a screwdriver."

Mike and Evan will be home any minute. Or will they? They might be trapped at the hospital with this tornado outside. She wondered what she'd more likely die from—the tornado, or Wes stabbing her. Instinctively, she crawled into the bath tub. She could no longer hear Wes pounding over the sound of the tornado. *Please, God, let me live through this.* Then, silence. The shaking walls were still. She listened for Wes. *He could be waiting right outside for me to open this door. How long should I wait here?* It seemed like hours. She was afraid to move.

Pounding on the bathroom door. Her heart stopped.

"Mom, it's me. Open up. Are you okay?"

"Evan? Yes, I'm okay." She unkinked her body and crawled out of the tub, then flung open the bathroom door and flew into Evan's arms.

"It's okay now The storm has passed."

"Wes? Where is he? He came after me with a knife."

Mike said, "I didn't see him. Why would he come after you?"

"He and his brother. His mother switched the records after the fire. Dr. Schmidt found out."

Evan ran from room to room. "He's in here." Susan and Mike followed Evan into the master bedroom. A dresser had fallen on top of Wes/Jake. Evan felt for a pulse. "He's dead."

Chapter 24

A hot shower and a good night's sleep did wonders. The tornado had clipped the edge of Evan's building and it would require repairs. They spent the night at the Holiday Inn down the street, which miraculously was completely unscathed.

They ate breakfast together at the buffet.

"I can't believe I was living with a murderer," said Evan. "And he could have killed you, too!"

"But he didn't. And in the end, he paid the price. I hope they arrest his mother too."

Mike said, "She was an accessory to murder plus switching those records? Of course they'll arrest her."

Susan said, "In all the commotion, I forgot to ask. What was the glitch with Mike's tests?"

"There wasn't a glitch. Wes made that call to get us out of the apartment. Dad is perfectly fine and cleared to travel."

"That's great news!"

Valerie came into the dining area. "Susan, thank God you're okay! I'm sorry you went through that alone."

"If it wasn't for you, Wes wouldn't have been caught. He'd have been on the next flight to Bismarck. I hope your daughter isn't angry at you."

"She'll get over it. If she stays mad, who's going to cart Elijah back and forth to school for her?"

"I'm going to miss you."

"Same here. We're two peas in a pod the two of us. I've always wanted to visit New York."

"You're welcome anytime. I'd love for you to visit. And we'll be back here in May for graduation."

"I'll start checking out Broadway shows. I'd love to see *Hamilton*! Meanwhile, take care." She gave her a hug and wished them a safe flight.

Mike went for more eggs.

"Evan, where are you going to live while they repair your place?"

"Cara said I could stay with her. My lease is up in June, and then Cara and I are going to look for a place together."

Susan smiled from head to toe. "Really?"

"Yeah. And there's one more thing I want before you and Dad head back to New York."

"What's that?"

"Can you come diamond shopping with me this afternoon?"

THE END

ABOUT THE AUTHOR

 Diane Weiner is a veteran public school teacher and mother of four children. She has enjoyed reading for as long as she can remember. She has fond memories of reading Nancy Drew and Mary Higgins Clark on snowy weekend afternoons in upstate New York and yearned to write books that would bring that kind of enjoyment to her readers. Being an animal lover, she is a vegetarian and shares her home with two adorable cats. In her free time, she enjoys running, attending community theater productions, and spending time with her family (especially going to the mall with her teenage daughter and getting Dairy Queen afterwards).

Murder Is Medical, is the tenth in Diane's Susan Wiles Schoolhouse mystery series. Diane also writes the Sugarbury Falls mysteries.

Visit dianeweinerauthor.com to find out more about the author.

OTHER BOOKS BY DIANE WEINER

Murder is Elementary

Murder is Secondary

Murder in the Middle

Murder is Private

Murder is Developmental

Murder is Legal

Murder is Collegiate

Murder is Chartered

Murder is Homework

A Deadly Course

Murder, of Course

Lightning Source UK Ltd.
Milton Keynes UK
UKHW011831231219
355918UK00001B/97/P